First published in the UK in 2018 by Nosy Crow Ltd
The Crow's Nest, 14 Baden Place, Crosby Row, London SE1 1YW
www.nosycrow.com

Nosy Crow and associated logos are trademarks and/or registered trademarks
of Nosy Crow Ltd

Printed and bound in the UK by Clays Ltd, St Ives Plc
Typeset by Tiger Media

Papers used by Nosy Crow are made from wood grown in sustainable forests.

ISBN: 978 1 78800 239 4

CONTENTS

FOREWORD

My older child was able to vote for the first time in the last election, and took a lot of pride in it. This brought home to me the importance of being able to vote, and when I discovered that the centenary of the date on which the first British women were given the vote was coming up, I thought that it deserved recognition.

And it was that idea which led to this book, *Make More Noise*. We decided to commemorate the hundredth anniversary of women's suffrage by creating a collection of brand new short stories by some of our favourite women writers, celebrating interesting and inspiring female characters.

Some of these stories have been inspired by real people and events from history, and others are entirely imagined, but what they all share is a celebration of girls and women at the centre of their own stories – in all kinds of different ways.

From Sally Nicholls' re-imagining of the night of the 1911 census, on which many women hid from their homes as a protest against their lack of voting rights, to Kiran Millwood Hargrave's magical parable of a world that's been flooded by a sea of witch's tears, there is something here for everyone. There are ghost stories, fairy tales, stories set in the present day, and stories set over a hundred years ago. Stories that will make you laugh, make you cry, make you think, and make you cheer.

We're so proud of the incredible collection of authors who have contributed to *Make More Noise*, and of the stories they have written.

And we're also especially happy to be partnering with Camfed for this book. Camfed is an international charity tackling poverty and inequality by supporting marginalized girls to go to school and succeed, and empowering young women to step up as leaders of change, and it felt particularly appropriate to be able to support these efforts with a book celebrating inspiring girls and women: £1 from the sale of every copy of *Make More Noise* will go directly to Camfed.

In the speech from which this book takes its name, Emmeline Pankhurst said: "You have to make more noise than anybody else, you have to make yourself more obtrusive than anybody else, you have to fill all the papers more than anybody else, in fact you have to be there all the time and see that they do not snow you under."

We hope that this book inspires you to make more noise.

Kate Wilson, Managing Director, Nosy Crow
February 2018

OUT
FOR THE
COUNT

*Sally
Nicholls*

The boys say it's jolly well not fair, and why should us girls have all the fun, and couldn't they come too? But Mummy says no. Tonight is for the women. Mummy and Enid and me, and Cook and Gladys and Miss Norcote, if they'd like to come.

Miss Norcote is our governess. Gladys is the maid. Gladys says, not likely! Not that she wouldn't like a vote, but she's that tired after a day's work, she's not about to go and sleep in a field to get it, thank you very much. But Cook says she's game, and so, rather surprisingly, does Miss Norcote. Miss Norcote is old – much older than Mummy and Daddy – and rather prim and buttoned-up-tight, so even Mummy's a bit taken aback when she says she'd like to come. But of course, Mummy just smiles and says that would be wonderful.

Mummy's a suffragette and so are Enid and I – or we would be, only there's not much call for suffragetting in Peasecombe, which is the village where we live. I *do* think it's unfair. In York and Leeds and London and places like that, suffragettes have a jolly old time of it going on marches, and throwing stones through shop windows, and getting flung into gaol. But there aren't any marches in Peasecombe, and there're only three shops, and we can't very well throw stones through their windows because they all know who we are, and if we started doing things like that we wouldn't have anywhere to buy bread, which would be dashed inconvenient. So mostly Mummy is just the sort of suffragette who writes letters to MPs and argues with Granny at Christmas.

But not today.

Tonight, April the second, 1911, is the census. That means the government wants to count how many people there are in Britain, just like in the Bible when Mary and Joseph had to go to Bethlehem to be counted, only here you stay in a house and you're counted there. But the suffragettes say that if women don't count in elections, we're jolly well not going to let them count us in the census either. So the idea is that women all over Britain aren't going to *be* in a house on census night, and that'll muck up the count and give the government no end of a headache.

Mummy has a subscription to *Votes for Women*, which is a newspaper, and it's full of all the things women are going to do tonight instead of stay at home. They've hired ice rinks and they're going to have all-night skating parties, and sleep in coal

3

sheds, and go off in gypsy caravans, and stay up all night reading plays in secret locations, and go walking on the moors, and do all sorts of things. There's even going to be an all-night concert for census-dodgers in Trafalgar Square. We haven't got anything like that in Peasecombe, of course, but Mummy says we're going to have a private protest. We're going to take our tents and pitch them on Ennesthwait Ridge, and we're going to cook our dinner on an open fire, and stay out till morning.

Enid and I think it's a topping way to protest.

"Just think if everyone did it!" says Enid. "That'd be one in the eye for the rotten old government! They'd *have* to give us a vote then."

★

Census night is a Sunday. We spend the morning fetching the camping things from the outhouse and packing them up into haversacks and the handcart. A few people stare as we walk through the village, but not many; we're always doing queer things in our family, so they're rather used to us.

As it comes out the other side of the village, the road begins to climb. After really not very long at all, you come to the edge of the woods, and almost immediately there's this little dirt track with a wooden signpost that says ENNESTHWAIT RIDGE, THE MOORS, like the ridge is a person and that's its address. As soon as we get under the trees, I feel excitement quickening in me. I look at Enid, and I know she feels it too. It's like we've left the village behind at last and the adventure's begun.

The track goes straight up the hill, and very quickly it stops being an adventure and starts being hard work. Ennesthwait Ridge isn't exactly *high* – I mean, we've been climbing it since we were little people of three or four – but this time, of course, we've got tents, and blankets, and food, and toothbrushes, and Enid's and my bicycle lamps (Mummy has an electric torch, oh, lucky, lucky Mummy), and pyjamas, and clean stockings, and matches, and the frying pan, and the little camping kettle, and tea towels, and dishcloths, and really, given that we're only staying one night, it's a beastly lot of things. Mummy and Cook take one of the handcart's handles each, and the rest of us put our backs to it, and it's *push – push – push* all the way up.

All the really heavy things are in the cart, of course, but we all have haversacks with our night things in them. We don't have much, but it's astonishing how much harder climbing is with things on your backs. It's also cold, though we quickly warm up with all the climbing. I hope we'll be all right tonight. Mummy's packed simply heaps and heaps of blankets, and if Captain Scott can camp in Antarctica, I suppose we can in April in Yorkshire. Even so, I'm beginning to worry a bit.

But then I remember the suffragettes like Mrs Pankhurst who go to prison and suffer all sorts of horrible torments, and I tell myself not to be such a weed.

It is ever such a beastly lot of up, though.

"Why do we have to camp *here*?" Enid wails.

Mummy looks a bit sheepish and says, "Oh, darling, I am sorry. I just thought it would be rather jolly, that's all. Daddy and Uncle James and I spent a night up here once – we lit a fire and stayed up all night until the sun rose. I thought we might pitch in the same place."

This, of course, puts all the climbing in a different light. "Rather!" I say.

And Enid says,

"Oh, won't the boys be sore they missed *this*?"

The side of Ennesthwait Ridge is mostly wooded. But then you come out on to the top, and it's moor as far as you can see, all purpley-green in summer and simply humming with bees. The path comes out of the wood and takes a sharp left along the side of the moor, and there's a little open space with rocks, and a bench, and a view of Peasecombe and all the valley spreading out beneath you. It's an A1 place to camp.

Usually when we camp, it's just the boys and Enid and me, in the wood at Grandfather's house in summer. We have two tents; one for Cecil and Nicholas and one for us girls. Miss Norcote and Cook will sleep in the boys' tent, but…

"Where are you going to sleep, Mummy?" says Enid. Mummy looks rather awkward.

"Well," she says. "I didn't exactly expect Miss Norcote and Cook to want to come. But don't worry about me. I'm going to get a big lot of wood together and sit up by the fire like Daddy and Uncle James and I did. That way I won't be worrying about how cold you all are."

"I say!" says Enid. "Are you really? May Jean and I stay up too?"

"Yes, may we?" I say.

Mummy hesitates. "Oh…" she says. "Well…"

"It would save us all heaps of work if we didn't

7

have to make up palliasses," I say.

Palliasses are sort of big bag things that you take camping, and you fill them up with straw or something, and then you've got something soft to sleep on.

Mummy smiles. "I think we'll make up the palliasses anyway," she says. "Then they'll be there if you change your minds."

But Enid and I know we won't.

✳

Have you ever been camping? It's the most ripping fun, but it's a frightful lot of work. First you have to put the tents up. Then you fill the palliasses. Ours are made of sacking, and we fill them with heather. Heather is simply the most glorious thing in the world to have in your bed, especially in summer. It's all springy and bouncy and it has the most heavenly honey-y smell. If I was a millionaire, I'd fill up all my mattresses with it, and sleep on it every night.

Mummy and Cook put up the tents, then go to help Miss Norcote cut the heather. Enid and I gather simply heaps of firewood and pile it up in a great big stack. Then we go help Mummy stuff the palliasses. But even then we aren't done.

Miss Norcote gets the sheets and blankets out of the handcart and makes up the beds.

Mummy sits down with a knife to cut a square of turf where we'll have the fire. Enid and I find two big forked sticks. Mummy drives them into the ground, one on either side of the fireplace, and we lay another big long stick across them like a medieval spit, so we can hang the kettle over the flames.

"Time for a cup of tea, I think," says Mummy, and she sends me running down to the beck to fill the kettle.

Oh, it *is* lovely, sitting there with the little yellow flames dancing in the fireplace, drinking tea and eating squares of Dairy Milk and looking out at Peasecombe and the fields all laid out like *The Land of Counterpane*. And isn't it funny seeing Miss Norcote sitting there on a boulder with her face all red from the heather-cutting and palliasse-stuffing, and a long streak of mud on her skirts? And Cook with her hat all askew, saying, "Eh… now this *is* a treat!"

I do like Cook. She's small and skinny, and full of tremendous energy. I *do* think it's ripping she's a suffragette.

We let the fire burn down, and then we start to cook. The older a fire is, the hotter it gets — did you know that? You want that deep, dark-red glow to cook on, not the early yellow flames. We push potatoes into the embers and we fry the sausages in the frying pan. We eat them with salt and mustard and lots of butter, and they're glorious, the very best sort of outdoor food, ever so much nicer than dull old sandwiches in packets of greaseproof paper. We finish up with a treacle tart that Cook made this morning and then we do the washing up. I'm frightfully glad Cook packed the washing-up bowl and some soap flakes twisted up in a bit of paper, because I never, never would have, and we'd have been scuppered without them. Then Mummy chucks a whole lot more wood on to the fire, and it throws up all these sparks, and it's just A1, and I wish we could eat on an open fire every day, like Taffimai's family do in the *Just So Stories*.

It's still cold, but it's much warmer sitting by the fire. We watch the sun set over the village.

It's ever so queer to think of all those families down there eating boring everyday suppers inside, while we're up here, swizzing the census and fighting for votes for women.

Miss Norcote says, "It's going to be dark soon, girls, so you'd better wash and brush your teeth while there's still light."

Enid tries to tell her we don't need to get ready for bed, since we aren't *going* to bed, but she should know it's no earthly use arguing with Miss N. We've left it a bit late, but Miss Norcote has Mummy's electric torch, and Enid and I have our bicycle lamps, which we light from a splint from the fire. We take the soapy, tooth-powdery water down to the beck, tip it out and hurry back. Even just in the time it's taken to wash, it's got so much darker. You can't really see the village houses now, just the lights from the street lamps and the house windows. There are the lights of Peasecombe, then great acres of blackness, which are fields and woods, then further out across the valley you can see the house lights of farmhouses and shepherds' huts, then right on the horizon there's the dull glow of Ennesthwait town.

"It's beautiful," I say. It is.

"Are we really going to stay up all night?" says Enid, and Mummy says we are. "Even Miss Norcote and Cook?" I say, and they look at each other.

"Well..." says Miss Norcote. "I'm not sure..."

"I'm not," says Cook. "Votes for women is all well and good, but I need my beauty sleep. I'm sure you don't expect me to cook for nine tomorrow on no sleep, ma'am, because I tell you now, it ain't going to happen."

And Mummy laughs and says of course she doesn't, and she's ever so grateful that Cook's even come at all.

It's half past eight, which is past Enid's bedtime already, but it's still quite early for the grown-ups, of course. Anyway, no one wants to go to bed just yet. We're all wrapped up in blankets, and winter coats, and hats and gloves and scarves, and two pairs of stockings, and two of our woolliest vests. Well, Enid and I are anyway.

Mummy puts the kettle on again and makes us all a cup of cocoa.

"I wish we could be suffragettes every night," I say, and Enid says she does too.

"And how perfectly scrumptious that Cook and Miss Norcote are suffragettes too!" she says. "*I* never knew you were a suffragette, Cook. Have you always been one and just never told us?"

Cook laughs. "Eh?" she says. "Me? Not likely!

Nay, but it's a cruel hard world to be a woman in, I do know that."

"*Is* it?" I say. Is Cook's life cruel and hard? I thought she liked working for us.

"Is it?" says Cook. "Why! What sort of lives do most women lead? Housework, and babbies, and worrying about your man – if you have one – and trying to keep the wolf from your door if you don't. Take my sister Gertie. She works at Ennesthwait Mill and earns half what a man does for doing the same job. Where's the fairness in that?"

"*Really?*" says Enid.

"Teaching's the same," says Miss Norcote. "A man has to support a family, but a woman only has to support herself. That's what they say. So she gets paid half the money for doing the same job."

There's a bitterness in her voice that I've never heard before. I'm horrified.

"The brutes!"

"Aye," said Cook. "And do they pay the widow more if *she* has a family to support? Do they heck!"

"No," says Miss Norcote. "It's almost impossible for a woman to provide for a family. I should know."

"You've got a family?" I say. "You've got *children*?"

13

Now I really am shocked. People who aren't married can't have children. It's... well, I don't know if it's against the law or what, but nobody does.

"You can't have children!" Enid says. "You're a Miss!"

"And don't I know it!" Miss Norcote says bitterly. "No, I don't have children. But once, a long time ago, I had a mother and a poor invalid sister. And when my dear father passed away, it was my duty to provide for them."

We stare. This is fascinating. I never thought of Miss Norcote as a *person*, not really. She's just... she's just *there*. Teaching us arithmetic, and mending our stockings, and telling us we have to finish our bread and butter before we eat our cake.

"What happened?" I say. "Couldn't you do it?"

"No, I managed it, just about. We sold our dear old house and moved to furnished rooms in Harrogate. My mother ran the house and I got a job teaching mathematics in a girls school. But it was a very difficult time. My sister needed so many things that we simply couldn't afford: doctors' bills, and special food, and rest cures at the seaside. She was twenty-six when she died, and I've often wondered..."

She stops, her voice choking. Enid puts out her hand. "Poor *darling* Miss Norcote," she says.

"I'm so sorry," Mummy says. "Unmarried women have it *so* hard, I always think."

A lot of women don't have husbands. Mummy says it's because so many men go out to India and Africa and places like that. Miss Norcote gives a most un-Miss-Norcote-ish snort. It's the only word for it.

"At least the unmarried woman can earn a living!" she says. "I had to refuse the only marriage proposal I ever received, because I simply couldn't look after Mother and Esther if I didn't have a job."

I'm agog. A love affair! A doomed love affair!

"Couldn't your husband look after them?" I say.

"Who was he?" says Enid.

Miss Norcote is shaking her head.

"He was the art master at the school where I taught," she says. "Knowing him – loving him – it was one of the greatest joys of my life. He asked me to marry him, and I wanted more than I've ever wanted anything to say yes. But it was impossible. A married woman can't be a teacher. And he had two little orphan brothers of his own to raise and educate. We could just about manage on two wages. But on one! It was impossible!"

"Oh, my dear," says Mummy. She seems to think that's the end of the story. But it can't be.

Why didn't they wait? They could have waited, surely?

"But when your mother and sister died," I burst out. "When his little brothers grew up...?"

"I couldn't have asked him to wait that long," Miss Norcote says simply. "It would have been years — a decade or more. He deserved more happiness than the sort of hole-and-corner romance I could have given him. I could bear my own unhappiness, but not his — never his! I told him he should forget me. He tried to argue, but in the end he did. He married a very nice girl. They had a family of their own, and I believe they were very happy."

We're quiet, looking out over the valley. Poor, poor Miss Norcote! Even Enid is silent.

Then Cook says, "Aye, the world is cruel hard on women. It's bitter cruel on mothers too. Take my other sister Susan, now. She were married to a terrible wicked fellow. Spent all the bairns' money on drink, and then came home and beat them black

16

and blue when the devil was in him. At last, Susan ran away, and she took the bairns with her and set herself up as a seamstress. Doing very well she was too, till her husband found out where they were. And then what do you think he did? Only took the bairns away, and gave them to his sister to raise! Said he's quite within his rights as their father, as she's the one 'as left him, and she's never to see them again!"

"No!" I say, shocked.

"Oh yes," says Cook. "Susan were beside herself, but the policeman said there were nothing to be done, since it were her what left him."

I can't believe it.

"Mummy, that *isn't* true? Is it?"

"Yes," says Mummy. She sounds sad. "Under English law, Susan's husband did nothing wrong. The mother has no rights to her children at all."

"But he can't stop her seeing them *forever*," says Enid. There are tears forming in the corner of her eyes. Mummy and Miss Norcote glance at each other, and I can see what Mummy's thinking: she shouldn't have let Cook say those things in front of Enid.

"No, of course he can't," I say hurriedly. Once

Enid gets upset, it takes her hours to calm down. "Don't be such a goose."

"She isn't being a goose," says Mummy. She turns and looks Enid straight in the eye, and there's something in the way she says the words that silences us. "It's a great injustice. It's an attack on a woman's very status as a human being. You're quite right to be upset, and Jean, you're quite right to be angry. But I'll tell you something." She takes Enid's chin in her hand and looks her in the eye. "Women everywhere are fighting this. We're coming together, and we're kicking, and we're shouting, and we're marching, and we're speaking, and we won't be silenced. And we *will* win. It might not be this year, and it might not be next, but it'll be soon. And when we win the right to be treated as citizens of this nation, we'll use our votes to fight all those battles that need winning. We'll make sure that children can't be taken from their mothers without due cause, and we'll make sure women get paid a fair wage for their work, and we'll fight until every town and village in England has lady doctors and lady lawyers and lady engineers and—"

"Lady train drivers," says Enid, and she giggles a little as she says it, so I know she's all right.

"And lady train drivers," says Mummy. "But if we want those things, it's women like us who'll have to do the fighting. These battles – they'll be won by ordinary people like you and me and Jean and Miss Norcote and Cook. What we're doing tonight is fighting for those children, Enid. Don't you ever forget it. And don't you ever give up."

"I won't!" says Enid. "I swear it!" She wipes her face with the back of her hand, and I'm surprised by how serious she sounds. My little sister Enid in her grubby pinafore and scuffed shoes and green hair ribbons. It's funny to think of Enid as a suffragette, fighting injustice, changing the world.

But why not?

Mummy's right. That's what we're doing, tonight.

✳

After Mummy's speech, Cook says she thinks it's time to turn in, and Miss Norcote agrees, rather hurriedly, as though she's regretting telling us all those private things about herself. We say our goodnights and they disappear to go to the lavatory and off to the boys' tent, and then it's just the three of us, Mummy and Enid and me.

"Sure you don't want to go to bed, girls?" says Mummy.

"No fear!" I say, and Enid agrees.

I want to talk about Cook, and Miss Norcote, and all the things they told us, but their tent is pitched right beside us and I'm worried they'll hear. Anyway, Mummy starts talking very briskly, as though she knows what I'm thinking and doesn't think it's quite the thing. Instead, she starts telling us all about the suffragettes in London, Mrs Fawcett and Mrs Pankhurst, and about marvellous women like Florence Nightingale and Mary Seacole, who looked after the poor soldiers in the Crimean War, and Mary Somerville, who studied complicated mathematics in secret and grew up to be one of the finest mathematicians of the age.

"Somerville College in Oxford is named for her," says Mummy. "I always rather hoped one of you girls, perhaps..."

"Me?" says Enid, astonished. "Not likely!"

"Well, Jean maybe," says Mummy. But *I* say I'd rather be a nurse on a front line somewhere and sew up men whose insides have been blown apart.

Mummy says, "You could be a doctor, like Dr Garrett Anderson," and I just stare, because I know there *are* lady doctors, but I never, never, never would have thought that one of them might be me.

Mummy laughs and says, "Shut your mouth before you swallow a fly. Whyever not? I simply longed to be a doctor when I was your age."

"*Did* you?" says Enid.

"I did," said Mummy. "You know Uncle James couldn't go to school because of his asthma. Grandfather didn't see why he should send me to school either, when he had a tutor right there in the house for James. So we used to do lessons together. I learned all sort of things girls aren't usually taught, like Latin and Greek and biology and chemistry. I thought perhaps I could be a doctor like Grandfather was."

My hat! I think. *I* never *knew that about Mummy.*

"Why didn't you?" I say, and her face tightens. If I didn't know better, I'd say she was angry. There's a strained edge to her voice.

"Oh," she says. "Grandfather wouldn't think of it. He thought lady doctors weren't ... respectable, I suppose. He wanted me to get married and have a family."

"Oh, Mummy, how perfectly horrid!" I say. "Why didn't you run away and be a doctor anyway? That's what *I* would have done."

"But how?" says Mummy. "It costs an awful

lot of money to go to university. If Grandfather wouldn't pay, how could I possibly afford it?"

I suppose she couldn't. I'm rather shaken. I always thought Mummy was happy. I mean, I know her life is rather dull — nothing to being a nurse on a front line, or an explorer like Cecil is going to be, or a train driver like Nicholas. But I thought she must like it well enough. Perhaps she doesn't. Perhaps she'd rather have been living another sort of life entirely.

Some of this must show in my face, because Mummy says, "Oh, darling! Don't look like that! It was ever such a long time ago. Why! If I'd been a doctor, I might never have married Daddy and had you children. And *then* where would I be?"

Enid looks comforted, but I'm not sure I am.

Given the choice between Daddy and Cecil and Enid and Nicholas and me, or this other life she might have been living…

Which would she have picked?

We sit quietly together for what feels like a long, long time, just watching the flames and thinking. My head is so full of new things to think about. I'm not at all sure I like it.

"Mummy," I say.

And Mummy says, "Yes, darling?"

"I *do* love you," I say.

And Mummy says, "I know, my love. And I love you too. I'm sorry about such a lot of things that have happened to me, but I've never been sorry about you children."

Enid says, "Mm-hmm," like she knew that already. She rests her head against Mummy's arm and closes her eyes. She's going to sleep. *I'm* not going to sleep though. I'm going to stay up all night with Mummy and watch the new day come in.

I'm just going to rest my eyes for a bit, that's all.

✷

I don't know how long I sleep for, but the next thing I know Mummy is shaking me gently, saying, "Jean… Enid… Wake up, darlings, look…" And I sit up and look, and the whole sky is this marvellous pinky-orangey-peachy colour, and it's full of all these little clouds in morning colours. It's one of the most beautiful things I've ever seen. And it's the sunrise, and it's April the third, and we've done it. We've swizzed the census.

Enid and I lean against Mummy, and she puts her arms around us, and we sit together under our blankets and watch as the sun comes up.

"I say," says Enid. "Do you think, next census, we'll have votes for women? When *is* the next census?"

"Nineteen twenty-one," says Mummy. It does sound ever such a long time away. What a lot of things might happen between now and then! Whatever *will* I be doing? I'll be twenty-one. Enid'll be eighteen. Cecil, poor fellow, will be twenty-three! A proper grown-up. "And yes," Mummy says. "I'm certain of it."

Enid gives a small, happy sigh. I put my head on Mummy's shoulder and watch the curls of smoke beginning to rise from the waking houses, and I wonder if she's right.

THE
BUG
HUNTERS

M.G.
LEONARD

Sofia's sigh misted up the car window as they drove down Brackenberry Road. She'd been hoping it would be a leafy dell or a forest glade, beside a river, with willow trees. She'd imagined number seven to be a thatched cottage, with foxgloves and hollyhocks, but Brackenberry Road was an ordinary street lined with ordinary houses, red-brick boxes topped with charcoal slate. The removal lorry farted grey smoke as it came to a halt outside an unremarkable house with the number seven on the door.

Sofia's mum parked the car behind the lorry and looked across at her from the driving seat.

"Wait till you see your new bedroom, Sofia," she said, her voice dancing with excitement. "You're going to love it here."

Sofia nodded, but she was doubtful. Saying goodbye to Jess, her best friend, knowing she wouldn't see her every day, had hurt. She'd cried for the first part of the car journey, until she'd run out of tears. She didn't want to move house, but Mum had got a new job and now everything had to change.

"I have to make sure the removal people put the boxes in the right rooms." Her mum pulled the keys from the ignition, dropping them into her handbag. "Why don't you explore the garden?"

"OK." Unclipping her seat belt, Sofia clambered out of the car. She was dressed for the outdoors, having got up early to take a last walk down the wildlife trail beside her old house and say goodbye to the forest den she and Jess had built from fallen branches and ferns. She was wearing her purple wellies with rainbow socks pulled up past her knees, a pink T-shirt covered in stars, and a pair of shorts that had once been jeans but had the legs cut off when Sofia had ripped them at the knees sliding down a muddy bank. She grabbed her blue hoodie and bug bag, pulling them both over her head as she walked towards the house.

Maybe the garden is overgrown and wild, with a pond full of frogspawn and newts, she thought. *There might be dragonflies.*

A woman in overalls was lowering a ramp at the back of the removal lorry. Two men inside the lorry were pushing boxes towards it. The door of number seven was already open. Sofia walked into the house, peering into the empty rooms. A staircase invited her upwards to see her new bedroom, but she ignored it, marching through the kitchen and out into a utility room where she found the back door. A silver key poked out of the lock.

This house may be horrid, she thought, *but the garden could be good.*

Sofia had dreamed of having a hidden, overgrown bit of earth to bring to life, ever since reading *The Secret Garden*. She turned the key and yanked the back door open.

A patio of concrete slabs led out to a long rectangle of perfectly mown grass. At the end of the garden, in the left-hand corner, was a neat-looking shed. Her curiosity dwindled as she approached it. The window in the door revealed that the shed was empty. There were three conifer trees at the bottom of the garden, their branches too dense with foliage for climbing. Sofia felt flat as she looked at the uninspiring garden, and a fire of anger tore through her chest.

"Urgh! I hate it here," she said to herself, kicking the trunk of the nearest conifer. "There aren't even any fruit trees!"

She watched as sticky sap oozed from the torn bark where her boot had struck the tree. "Oh, I'm sorry. It's not your fault."

She leaned her head against the bark, breathing

in the grassy-pine perfume of the wounded conifer. Her sore heart was throbbing like a thumb hit by a hammer. She wanted to go home. A tear ran down her cheek, but she wiped it away. She'd promised her mum she wouldn't cry any more.

A trail of determined ants, marching up the trunk of the injured tree, stopped to examine the freshly bled sap.

"Hello." Sophie brought her face close. "You're busy, aren't you?" Rummaging around in her bug bag, she pulled out a portable magnifying glass and slipped it out of its worn leather case. She crouched down and examined the army of ants.

Maybe now we've moved, she thought, *Mum will let me build an ant farm.*

With her head against the tree trunk she could see the fence at the back of the garden and there, tucked behind the empty shed, was a tall, thin gate.

"Oh!" She ducked under a low branch and wriggled through to the gap behind the shed. The gate was hidden from the rest of the garden. She drew back the bolt, but the door was swollen stuck. A couple of good shoves popped it open, and Sofia stepped out on to a footpath that ran along the back of the houses. It was wide enough to ride a bike down. On the opposite side of the footpath was a hedgerow, thick with nettles and brambles, and beyond it, a field of wheat.

"Blackberries!" Sofia stepped forward and picked one, popping it into her mouth, savouring the sour sweetness as it burst on her tongue. She walked along the hedgerow, picking and eating berries, until she noticed three caterpillars on nettle leaves close to the ground. She squatted down and peered at them through her magnifying glass. The caterpillars were nearly three centimetres long, dark with pale-tipped spines and a lemon pattern of marks along their bodies.

"*Vanessa atalanta*," she whispered to herself, opening her bag and pulling out a clear plastic pot with tiny air holes in the lid. Grasping the nettle leaf firmly with thumb and forefinger, to avoid being stung, she plucked the leaf hosting one of the caterpillars and carefully slid it into her pot.

Hearing a rustle, Sofia looked to her right. There was a girl, way up the path. She was standing feet apart, staring at Sofia, her eyes enlarged by thick glasses. She was wearing fluffy monster-feet slippers and a faded yellow adult-sized T-shirt as a dress with a belt pulling it in at the waist. In one hand she clutched a pad of paper, and in the other, a pencil case. Her long blonde hair looked like it hadn't been brushed in months.

Sofia lifted her hand and waved, but the girl turned and ran away.

"What are you doing?"

Sofia jumped, not expecting to hear a voice so close behind her. She spun round. Peering over the fence, a shrub of red curly hair sat atop two bright-blue eyes and a freckle-smattered nose.

"I'm bug hunting," Sofia replied, holding up her plastic pot. "This is the red admiral caterpillar. It's in its fifth instar, which means it's going to pupate soon and turn into a butterfly."

"Bug hunting?" With a scuffle and a thump, the red-haired girl was over the fence and crouching down beside her. "What are you hunting them for? Do you kill them?"

"No!" Sofia said. "That would be cruel."

"When people hunt animals they normally do kill them," the red-haired girl replied, staring down at the caterpillar in the pot. "They shoot them and chop off their heads, stuff them and hang them on the wall." She giggled. "Imagine hanging a dead caterpillar head on the wall."

Sofia frowned. She didn't like that idea.

"I live at number thirteen." The girl pointed at the house beyond the fence. "You're the new girl at number seven, aren't you?" She looked proud, as if she'd solved a mystery. "I saw you arrive."

"My name's Sofia."

"Hi, Sofia. I'm Cassidy." She pointed at the spiny caterpillar in the pot. "If you don't kill the bugs, what do you do with them?"

"Well, this one I was going to take back to my terrarium and watch it weave leaves together with silk, to make a cocoon. Then hopefully it will become a pupa and I'll see it transform into a butterfly." Sofia smiled, but Cassidy's expression was confused. "Other bugs I pick up and let them walk on me while I look at them with my magnifying glass." She slid the lens out for Cassidy to see. "You can see every detail, their compound eyes and hairy bodies."

"And then what?"

"I let them go." Sofia carefully put a lid on the pot containing the caterpillar and lowered it into her bug bag.

"Do you do it with all bugs?" Cassidy's face twisted. "Even spiders?"

"Oh yes," Sofia replied. "I love spiders. They're so beautiful."

"You let spiders crawl on you?" Cassidy stared at Sofia, aghast. "That's weird."

"No it isn't. It's natural."

"Well, if it's natural, then how come I've never met anyone else who does it?"

Sofia shrugged.

A male voice called, "Cassidy, dinner time. CASSIDY? WHERE ARE YOU?"

"That's my dad." Cassidy got up. "I've got to go. Will you be going to Bracken Heath School on Monday?"

Sofia nodded.

"Me too. See you there," Cassidy said, as she clambered over the fence and vanished.

✱

"Good morning, children," Miss Magister said in a high wavering voice.

"Good morning, Miss Magister," the children chanted back from behind their desks.

"We have a new person joining our class today. Her name is Sofia Elvidge." Miss Magister put her hand on Sofia's shoulder and gave her a watery smile. "Welcome, Sofia." She looked out into the class. "Now, who's going to volunteer to look after Sofia this week and show her around our school?"

Sofia saw the girl from the alleyway with the monster slippers put her hand up. Her blonde hair was scraped up into a tangled pineapple ponytail, her glasses had tape around one of the arms and her cardigan was buttoned up wrong, hanging off one shoulder to show a paint-splattered school blouse. There was an empty desk beside her.

Miss Magister looked at Cassidy, who had her hand up too. "Ah, Cassidy, thank you, that's very kind. Sofia, go and sit beside Cassidy. Mark, you can come over here and sit beside Beatrice."

"Do I have to, miss?" Mark complained as he scraped his chair backwards. "She smells of cabbages."

Miss Magister gave Sofia a gentle shove towards Cassidy.

Cassidy was looking about her, smiling victoriously. Her red hair was tied back neatly with a royal-blue ribbon and her white school shirt had pretty capped sleeves. She looked perfect.

"Hi." Sofia smiled as she sat down beside her new friend.

"Don't get too comfy," Cassidy whispered.

"Mark will want his chair back next week. He's my boyfriend."

"Oh, OK."

During the lesson Sofia didn't talk to Cassidy, who was preoccupied with writing and passing notes that seemed to be very funny. They were supposed to be answering questions about a book called *The Odyssey* that everybody except Sofia had read. The characters' names were strange, and Sofia was confused by the story. Once or twice she looked at Cassidy, hoping for help, but she was teasing Mark for having to sit next to Beatrice Beckett.

When the lunch bell went, Sofia got up in time to see Mark stick his foot out and trip Beatrice as she rose from her desk.

"Oops, clumsy bumble Bea!" Cassidy laughed.

Mark grinned as he came to stand beside Cassidy and they were joined by a girl called Amanda.

Beatrice scrambled to her feet, picking up her glasses from the floor. She looked up at Sofia, who blushed and looked down. She knew she should say something, but it was her first day at school and Cassidy – who appeared to be the most popular girl in the class – seemed to like her. When she looked up, Beatrice had gone.

"Why does your hair look like that?" Amanda asked Sofia.

"Like what?" Sofia put her hand up to the back of her head. Amanda had shiny brown hair in two long plaits.

"Short, like a boy's. Did you get punished?"

"No. I like it like this," Sofia explained. "My mum says I look like a pixie."

Mark snorted. "A boy pixie."

"C'mon, let's go to the canteen." Cassidy hooked her arm through Sofia's. "I'm starving."

"Oh, me too." Sofia smiled with relief at the change of subject.

When they got to the canteen, Cassidy paraded to the front of the dinner queue. "Excuse me, coming through," she trilled. "Got the new girl here." Sofia's face burned as everyone turned to look, but Cassidy loved the attention. She made a great show of getting Sofia a tray and explaining how to choose what you wanted to eat.

"Aren't you kind, duckie." A dinner lady smiled at Cassidy.

Sofia felt self-conscious with everyone staring at her. When they sat down to eat, a steady stream of children came over to talk to Cassidy, but they were looking at her.

Amanda pinched Sofia's arm. "Cassidy says you like creepy-crawlies. Is that true?"

"Oh yes." Sofia nodded. "I'm a naturalist."

Mark sprayed his drink all over the table and choked as he laughed. "*You walk around in the nude?*"

"NO!" Sofia was horrified. "That's *naturists*! I'm a *naturalist*. I study nature."

"You go outdoors, *naked*," Amanda gasped. "*And pick up bugs!*"

A ripple of whispers travelled across the dinner hall, heads turned and Sofia's insides burned. "I do *not* go around naked!" she cried out.

"Guys, people are staring at us." Cassidy raised an eyebrow.

"Sorry, Cass," Amanda said.

Sofia looked around the hall. People were pointing at her and giggling. "Now everyone thinks I'm a weird nudist," she said mournfully.

"I know how to fix this," Cassidy said brightly. "You can do the Show and Tell on Thursday."

"Show and Tell?" Sofia said.

"Yes, once a week, two people in the class have to bring in something to do with their hobbies and talk about it in form time. It's meant to be me and Jack Harrington this week. I was going to do it on ballet but, if you wanted, I could let you go instead of me."

"How's that going to help?"

"It will give people a chance to get to know more about you, and," she lowered her head and whispered, "you can explain that you're a naturist who likes bugs."

"But I'm *not* a naturist; that's a nudist!" Sofia felt panic fizzing in her chest like a hive of swarming bees. "I'm a *naturalist*."

"Exactly." Cassidy put her arm around Sofia's shoulder. "I know that, but they don't." She gestured to the dinner hall. "You don't want people thinking you walk around in your birthday suit at weekends, do you?"

Sofia shook her head.

"Good, then it's agreed." Cassidy clapped. "I'll tell Miss Magister you'll do the Show and Tell in my place."

✹

"Hey, wait for me," Sofia called out, running to catch up with Cassidy, Amanda and Mark, who were walking out of the school gate. They couldn't have heard her, because they didn't slow or turn around, and were nearly at the end of the road by the time she reached them.

"Oh, it's you," Cassidy said, as if she was surprised to see Sofia.

"Did you talk to Miss Magister about the Show and Tell?" Sofia asked, a little out of breath.

"Yes." Cassidy nodded. "You're doing it this week."

"Great," Sofia replied, glancing at Amanda and Mark, who were looking in any direction but hers. "Thanks."

They walked along in silence, Amanda, Cassidy and Mark spreading out to fill the pavement so that Sofia had to trip along in the gutter.

"Oh, look," Sofia called out, pointing at a bush hanging over the pavement in front of them. "What a beautiful cross-orb weaver."

Amanda, Mark and Cassidy didn't appear to hear her, and walked on as if she hadn't made a sound.

Sofia stopped. They were ignoring her! Before she could say anything, Amanda screamed and started leaping about.

"Aaaaarghhhhhh! I walked into a web! Is there a spider on me?" She threw her arms up and shook her head as Cassidy and Mark leapt back. "Is it on me?" she shrieked. "Can you see it?"

Sofia spotted the unfortunate spider clinging on to Amanda's hair as she bucked and flicked her plaits like a wild horse.

"I can see it," Sofia said calmly.

"Aaaarrrrghhhhhhhh!" Amanda screamed louder.

"If you stand still, I'll rescue it." Sofia stepped forward. "It's in your hair."

"Where is it?" Amanda whipped her chestnut braids about in a panic. "Get it off!"

"Stand still," Sofia ordered, reaching up and cupping her palms under the spider, coaxing it into her hands. She stepped away. "I've got it. It's OK. It's not hurt."

Amanda stumbled backwards. "Get away from me!"

"Calm down, Amanda, it's harmless." Sofia opened her hands a crack. "Look."

Amanda screamed.

"Stop it! You're bullying her." Cassidy scowled at Sofia. "Look how upset she is. You should apologise."

"What?" Sofia blinked. "But I took the spider off her, didn't I? You and Mark were going to run away."

"We were not!" Cassidy huffed. "She's lying, Amanda. I'd never leave you."

"It's OK to be scared of spiders," Sofia said. "But if you learned a little about them you'd see that they're wonderful creatures."

"I'm not scared of spiders." Mark lunged forward and shoved Sofia hard. She stumbled backwards, her hands opening to break her fall as she hit the pavement, and the spider dropped to the ground. In a flash, Mark lifted up his foot and stomped on the spider, squashing it dead. "See, I killed it."

"Oh!" Sofia's eyes filled with tears. "What did you do that for?"

"Because spiders are gross, and *you're* gross." Mark folded his arms across his chest.

"What kind of a girl likes bugs anyway?" Cassidy said, looking at Sofia with disgust.

"A freak," Amanda replied with a sneer.

Sofia wanted to shout something mean back, but her throat closed and her vision blurred as she fought with her tears. She didn't want them to see her cry.

"If you come near us again," Mark said, "I'll stamp on you, just like that spider."

As they walked away, Amanda chanted a limerick.

"There is a girl called Sofia,
so gross you'll scream if you see her.
She is covered in bugs,
cockroaches, spiders and slugs,
So steer clear of freaky Sofia!"

A tinkling laugh rose from Cassidy.

Sofia wiped her eyes with her sleeve and knelt forward to look at the poor crushed spider. "Poor little spinner," she sniffed. "You won't be making any more webs. You're nothing but bird food now." She lifted the mangled spider's body on to the hedge of the neighbouring garden, for a hungry bird to find.

✱

"Do I have to go to Bracken Heath School?" Sofia asked her mum the next morning at breakfast.

"Is there something wrong with the school, Sofia?" Her mum looked concerned. "People say it's a good one."

"No, I was just wondering if there was a different school I could go to." Sofia stared down into her cereal bowl. "You know, if I don't get along with the other kids."

"Is everything OK, pickle?"

Sofia nodded. "I miss Jess."

"I know you do, but you'll make friends at Bracken Heath. Just give it some time."

"What if I don't?" Sofia looked up. "Can we go home?"

"We are home." Her mum gave her a worried smile.

Sofia pushed her breakfast away. She wasn't hungry.

✶

Cassidy, Amanda and Mark were waiting for Sofia at the end of the road. They acted like she was invisible, until she had walked past. Then they followed her.

"Do you think she walks like that because she has ants in her pants?" Cassidy said.

"I bet she had to get all her hair cut off because she lets nits live in it," Amanda said.

"Her only friends are the *bugs*, cockroaches, spiders and *slugs*," Mark chanted.

Sofia tried to ignore them, and carried on walking as if they weren't there. On the other side of the road she saw Beatrice Beckett walking to school.

I bet she's happy they've got a new girl to pick on, Sofia thought.

43

She felt a hand on her back, and a push sent her stumbling forwards.

"Errrrrr," Amanda squealed. "Don't touch her! She's probably got diseases from maggots."

When she walked through the school gates, Sofia's heart was heavier than lead. She told herself that she just had to get through the day, one lesson at a time. Cassidy ignored her during class, which wasn't too bad. At break time, two kids she'd never met threw handfuls of earth at her and ran away. She sat on her own at lunch and overheard Cassidy boasting loudly about how she'd got out of having to do the Show and Tell by tricking the new girl into doing it. Sofia missed Jess and her old home so much her insides ached.

When the school bell rang at the end of the day, Sofia hurried out of the gate, keen to get home before Cassidy, Amanda and Mark could find her, but she heard Amanda's voice calling to Mark, so she dodged into the front garden of the nearest house, ducking down behind the hedge. As they passed by, Sofia overheard their conversation.

"Did you see where she went?" Mark was asking. "I thought she was in front of us."

44

"Maybe her mum picked her up in a car," Amanda said.

"No, her mum works," Cassidy replied. "She must have run home, scared." She laughed nastily.

"I thought I might join in Sofia's Show and Tell tomorrow," Amanda said. "I'm going to faint when she starts talking about her disgusting bugs."

"I don't understand how she can touch those horrible creepy-crawlies." Cassidy shivered. "There's something wrong with her."

"If she brings bugs into the classroom," Mark said, "I'm going to kill them all." Through the hedge, Sofia saw Mark pull a canister from his pocket. "Bug spray."

They laughed, their voices fading as they walked up the street.

Sofia stayed kneeling on the ground until she was certain they were gone. She shuffled home, her stomach whirling like a black hole as she thought about her Show and Tell tomorrow.

"I'm back," she called, going straight up the stairs to her bedroom, still filled with unpacked boxes.

"I'm just making dinner, pickle," her mum called.

Sofia walked into her bedroom, lifted her plastic terrarium off the window ledge and carried it downstairs, out of the back door, through the garden and into the alleyway behind the house. She pulled the lid off.

"Off you go," she whispered to the tiny invertebrates inside. "Be free. I'm not collecting bugs any more." She walked back to the house, leaving the terrarium behind.

✶

"Mum, I don't feel well," Sofia called out as her mum rushed passed her bedroom doorway, getting ready for work.

"Really? Oh, Sofia." She came in and put her hand on Sofia's head. "You're not hot. What's wrong?"

"I feel sick," Sofia lied.

"But you haven't been sick?"

"No, but I might be."

"Well, I have to go into work for a meeting. Go to school and if you don't feel good, go to the nurse and she can call me."

"Can't I stay here?" Sofia sank down into the duvet. "I don't mind if you leave me on my own all day."

"Sofia, you're eleven years old. I will not leave you on your own. Anyway, you might feel better once you're on your feet. Get up and get dressed."

Her mum scurried out of the room, pulling on a shoe.

Sofia sighed and swung her legs out of bed. She wasn't completely lying. She did feel sick, because today was Show and Tell.

✱

"Right, children, after I've taken the register, we'll move on to today's Show and Tell," said Miss Magister.

"Miss, miss!" Jack's hand went up. "I can't do my Show and Tell. I forgot my bag."

"Well, it will just be a 'tell' then, won't it?" Miss Magister looked over her glasses at him.

"But, miss, I was going to do mine on ... stamp collecting."

A giggle zipped around the classroom.

"It would be boring without the actual stamps." Jack smiled, pleased with himself.

Miss Magister sighed. "Oh, very well, you can do yours next week. Sofia, you'll have a bit longer to talk about your hobby. Now, I'm going to read the register and I'd like you to say 'here' in a nice loud voice when I call your name."

As the voices rang out, Sofia's ears filled with buzzing.

"Sofia Elvidge. Sofia Elvidge?"

"Oh, sorry. Here, miss." Her voice sounded small. She wondered if she was going to faint, and thought that would be good, because then she wouldn't have to stand up in front of everybody. She closed her eyes and silently told her body to faint. But when she opened her eyes she was still sitting in her chair next to Cassidy.

"Right, now, Sofia, come to the front of the class and set up any props you want to use to show and tell us about your hobby."

Sofia swallowed. "I – I – I didn't bring anything," she whispered, looking at the ground.

"Come now, we've had this excuse already, from Jack. Up you come."

"Don't worry, Sofia," Mark called out. "I brought you something."

Sofia felt something hit her cheek and clatter to the desk. She looked down. It was a dead beetle – a rust-brown chafer.

"Ew!" Cassidy squealed, pushing her chair back. "It's a cockroach!"

There were three or four gasps and squeals, and more chairs moving away, as Sofia tenderly picked up the beetle.

"Is it alive?" Miss Magister looked nervous.

"Nah, miss, it's dead." Mark leered at Sofia. "I killed it with my bug spray."

"Oh, OK then. Calm down, everybody. Go back to your seats. Yes, Beatrice, what do you want?"

Beatrice was standing at the front of the classroom with a big cloth sack, out of which she pulled a folded-up easel and a board with a picture on it.

"I'm going to do my Show and Tell, miss." She pushed her glasses up her nose. "Everyone else has forgotten their things, but I brought mine."

"Oh, right. Well, I suppose that's OK." Relieved, Miss Magister retreated behind her desk. "Sofia, you can go after Beatrice."

Everyone had stopped staring at Sofia, and now they watched Beatrice Beckett setting up her easel.

"Today I want to tell you about Maria Sibyl Merian," Beatrice said. "She was born over three hundred years ago in Germany and she is so important that her face used to be on their money. She was a scientific illustrator." She pointed at the picture on the easel. "She painted pictures of nature. This is one of her pictures."

It was a coloured plate torn from an old book.

A stag beetle with wings spread wide flew above a plant with flowering white bells. On the leaves were a plump cream larva and a black weevil, and below them hung two green fruit, one hosting a caterpillar, the other attracting a bee.

"Her pictures are so famous that the Tsar of Russia and King George III of England bought them. The reason she is such an important lady is because she started collecting caterpillars at the age of thirteen and was so fascinated by how they changed into butterflies that she learned to paint, to tell their story. She was the first scientist to capture the metamorphosis of insects and she published a book about it, which changed how people looked at invertebrates." She took a deep breath and continued.

"But also, because all other scientists and artists were men, she wasn't taken seriously. She sold all her possessions and took her daughter on an expedition to Suriname, to collect and draw the flora and fauna she found there. She was very brave to do this in a time when only men did these things, and people thought her interest in insects strange." Beatrice looked at Sofia. "She was an adventurer and I think she is wonderful. She is my favourite artist." She smiled. "Back then, hundreds of years ago, people thought insects weren't important and that girls weren't important either, and that girls definitely should not like insects and be studying them or painting them." Beatrice turned her head and looked Cassidy straight in the eye. "Thank goodness times have changed and we all know what a stupid way of thinking that is." She turned back to the picture she'd brought with her. "When I grow up I want to be an artist, so I spend as much time as I can painting outside and looking at nature, to get really good, like Maria Merian." She paused and said in a loud clear voice, "And I think if we want to discover the secrets of life and make something important, we shouldn't listen to people that tell us what we are supposed or not supposed to do." Beatrice did a funny bow. "The end."

Miss Magister clapped and stood up. "Well, that was very interesting, Beatrice, and quite profound."

Everyone in the classroom applauded, but Sofia most of all.

"Now, Sofia, would you like to come up and tell the class about your hobby."

"Oh!" Sofia's hands dropped.

"Is it OK if I help her?" Beatrice asked, bending

down and lifting Sofia's plastic terrarium out of her large cloth bag.

"My bugs!" Sofia was so surprised that she rose from her seat and moved to the front of the class without a thought for the eyes on her. She peered into the terrarium. All her friends were in there – the cricket, the caterpillar munching on the nettle leaf, the woodlice and her babies on a rotting bit of bark, and the violet ground beetle scrambling around in the corner. She was pleased to see them.

"Miss Magister, when I first saw Sofia, she was collecting caterpillars just like Maria Merian," Beatrice said. "Isn't that wonderful?"

Sofia turned to face the classroom. "My hobby is that I like to explore the countryside, hunting for different types of invertebrates, and study them to learn about them. Invertebrate means a creature that doesn't have a spine. Instead they have an exoskeleton – a skeleton on the outside of their body – but they get called bugs, creepy-crawlies or mini-beasts by most people."

The classroom was silent. Everybody's eyes were fixed on the terrarium.

"Where I used to live, at the weekends me and my best friend Jess would go out on bug hunts with our butterfly nets, collecting jars, and magnifying glasses. We'd catch different types of insects, bring them home to look at and add into our nature diaries, then set them free. My favourite type of creatures are moths, because they are the funkiest-looking caterpillars. People think moths are ugly, but if you look at them under a microscope they have amazing patterns. They look like tiny hairy muppets with crazy long curly tongues."

A ripple of laughter disturbed the quiet classroom. Sofia smiled at Beatrice, who smiled back.

"Some people think it's weird for a girl to like bugs, but there shouldn't be rules about what girls or boys can like. I hope by looking at insects and learning about nature, I will be able to do good things for the environment when I grow up."

"In here are lots of invertebrates that Sofia's captured on bug hunts," Beatrice said, pointing at Sofia's terrarium. "Who wants to see?"

And suddenly everyone was out of their desks and crowding round the tank.

"Look, a cricket."

"Oh, look, teeny-tiny baby woodlice, and they're white!"

"What's that on the lavender?"

"It's a leaf beetle," Sofia replied. "Sometimes called a rosemary beetle. Isn't it pretty?" Glancing over the heads of her excited classmates, Sofia saw that the only people still sitting at their desks were Cassidy, Mark and Amanda.

At the end of the day, Sofia waited for Beatrice and they walked home together, one girl carrying a terrarium full of bugs and the other with a cloth bag slung over her shoulder.

"Thanks for saving my terrarium," Sofia said. "It must have been heavy to bring to school."

"My mum helped me," Bea said. "I knew you couldn't really want to throw it away."

"Do you think, maybe, you might like to go on a bug hunt with me one weekend?" Sofia asked.

"Oh!" Beatrice flushed pink. "I'd love to. I know this great place by the river where there's dragonflies, big red ones."

"There's a river?"

"Yes, at the other end of Brackenberry Road the footpath at the back of the houses leads to a glade of willow trees beside a river. I'm building a den there. You could help me, if you like?"

Sofia beamed. "I'd like that a lot."

ALL THINGS BRIGHT AND BEAUTIFUL

PATRICE LAWRENCE

Angel's hair was full of spiders. That's the first thing I remember about that day. I'd thought they were ants, but I should have known. I'd dug out enough ants' nests in the dry earth down by the canal. These were what Nanna called penny spiders, tiny things, running down Angel's forehead and cheeks in a quick, grey stream, dodging my hands as I tried to sweep them off her. But I didn't want to squash them. It wasn't their fault that they'd made their home in the wrong place. Nanna's bonnet must have looked so tempting and it had been empty for months.

"Take it off, Angel!"

My sister was sitting on our bed, hunched against the damp wall, her arms hanging by her sides. Her mouth was a little bit open and I was frightened that the spiders would run inside. She was two years older than me but was always smaller. Nanna said they never expected her to live. She'd got measles and diphtheria but she'd beaten them both. She'd been stronger than they'd thought.

"Angel?"

Her eyes were closed and she was shaking. I lifted the bonnet off her head and checked inside. I brushed away a few wisps of web, but all the spiders were gone. If they really wanted to escape, it was easy. They could hide in the cracks that spread across the wall, or scuttle out of the missing windowpane, or race into the cold fireplace and up the chimney. They could even go out the way we did, through the door-shaped hole into the hallway.

"You have to check your clothes, Angel!"

She opened her eyes and looked at me as if she was going to say something, then she slid down on to the bed, scrunching herself up like newspaper.

"This is no place for the idle!"

Mrs Vickery was standing where the door should be. She was so big she could have *been* the door, blocking out the dark hallway behind her. She wrinkled her face at the stink. I should have emptied the chamberpot first thing, but I'd been too worried about Angel. Though the smell from the privy in the yard outside was blasting through the room anyway.

"Angel isn't lazy," I said. "She's still sick."

Mrs Vickery's face wrinkled even more. "She isn't sick. She's idle. I told you, I got a respectable family ready for this room. They paid me up front."

I glanced over at Angel. Her face was turned to the wall. I bit down on my lip. *Respectable?* I wanted to yell. *Your last "respectable" family ran out after chopping up the door for firewood. They didn't even leave us any.*

I said, "You'll have our rent tomorrow."

Mrs Vickery's mouth twitched. "You said that yesterday."

"I know. But Angel's sick."

"Sick in the head. Just like your mother."

My teeth dug deeper. Soon there'd be blood. "We'll have your money tomorrow, Mrs Vickery."

"And how do I know she isn't going to be sick tomorrow?"

Mrs Vickery looked around the room, at the bottles with the candle wax dribbling down the sides, past the small blue globe that was Nanna's and then Mama's. I'd found some apples in the market yesterday and tried to coax Angel to eat one. She'd taken a small bite and stuck it back in the bowl. The flesh had gone all brown.

Mrs Vickery shook her head. Her black bonnet shuffled. I hoped the spiders had sneaked along the thick folds of her neck and up into her hair.

She said, "I only let you stay so long because your grandmother was a respectable woman. Such a pity your mother brought her so low."

I moved back towards Angel. I wanted my body

to block out the words that I knew were coming.

Mrs Vickery leaned back against the crooked doorframe. "She did her best, your grandmother. But your mother…"

I dug my nails into my leg but the words burst out. "Nanna loved us!"

Mrs Vickery's eyebrows shot up. Her bonnet jerked back. "She was a decent woman. She did her best." She shook her head again. "And do you know what I told her?"

"Stop it!" I glanced back at Angel. The words usually hit her hard, because she remembered our father. For me, he was like a ghost, almost real, but just out of my sight.

Mrs Vickery laughed. She sounded like the night cats that squawked beneath our windows.

"I told her that the best thing your father could have done was take you with him back to whatever country he came from!"

Trinidad, I wanted to whisper. Grandma had drawn a tiny little circle round it on the globe.

Mrs Vickery rubbed her hands. "For your grandmother's sake, I'll give you until six o'clock tonight. It won't be me coming for the money. It will be Bernard. He's not as kind as I am."

She turned and swished away.

Bernard, with his twisted nose and his eyes that were always half closed and swollen. Sometimes he'd appear as Angel and I left our room in the morning. He'd never speak to us. He'd just stand there, filling the hallway. He'd crack his knuckles and grin, showing the jagged teeth in his big, dark mouth. His nails were rimmed with dirt and blood from working in the slaughterhouse. We'd squeeze past, holding our breath so we didn't breathe in the smell of dying animals.

I crouched next to Angel and shook her. "Can you get up today? We're going to be out on the street!"

Angel crumpled herself together even more.

"Angel?"

"Vicky. I'm so sorry. I just can't... I should be with Mama. Please let me go."

"No, Angel. You have to stay with me."

She was crying again. I dabbed away the tears with the corner of my skirt. "We'll be all right. I promise."

I pulled our blanket over her. She didn't move. I poured some water into a bowl, dipped in a rag and rubbed my face. It probably didn't make much difference. I needed a proper wash. I should borrow Mrs Sweeting's bath and try and find some coal to boil the water. But not now. Because I had made a promise and I had until six o'clock to keep it.

I kissed Angel's forehead. "I'll be back soon."

Her eyes flicked open and she grabbed my arm. "Don't leave me, Vicky."

"I have to."

"No." She clung on tighter.

I stroked her hand and lay down on the bed next to her. When Mama was ill, there was only one way Nanna could calm her down. I closed my eyes and tried to push the dark things out of mind and fill it with birds singing and flowers opening and icicles hanging from winter branches.

I took a deep breath and started to sing:

"*All things bright and beautiful. . .*"

Slowly, her hand relaxed. I touched her cheek. Her breath was slow and shallow. She sighed. I hoped she was dreaming about sunsets and mountains.

I sat on the edge of the bed and squeezed my feet into Angel's boots. They didn't leak as much as mine. I pulled on Nanna's old coat and crept downstairs and out of the front door.

Monday was washday. Lines were looped across

our narrow street from window to window, clothes and sheets flapping in the wind. Mrs Sweeting was outside prodding a mound of laundry in her tin bath. Laura, her oldest, was sitting on the step singing to a tiny baby tucked into an old fruit crate next to her. I smiled at them; Laura made a face back.

"Do you need any help?" I asked.

"Nothing for you today, darling." Mrs Sweeting nodded towards the bundle in the crate. "I need every penny now. Sorry."

I forced out another smile but tears prickled behind. She was the only one who'd give me a few pennies to help her. None of the other women would meet my eyes. They knew how close they were to being like us.

I'd have to try Mrs Kastner. I cut through the alleyways, skirting round the back of the goods yard, passing through St Leonard's churchyard into Hackney Road. The fog was hanging heavy; I could taste it.

Mrs Kastner and her daughter, Rebecca, owned a sweet shop. The windows were so clean I could almost touch the jars of liquorice and pear drops. Sometimes I'd help Rebecca polish the glass panes and she'd give me a couple of pennies. Even better were the toffees, as hard as bones, wrapped in a twist of paper. I could make one last nearly an hour. But the shop door was still locked. That was unusual.

Mr Kastner's furniture shop was next door. He and his two brothers made tables and chairs in the workshop out the back. It was dusty, messy work and if they were really busy, they'd let me and Angel sweep up. We'd get enough for bread and tea, and wood shavings for our fire. But their shop was locked too. I glanced down the road. Only a few shops were open.

I crossed over to Mr Mackenzie's butcher's. Strings of fat sausages hung from hooks behind the counter. Thick joints of meat sat on trays waiting for customers to take them away — customers with money. Mrs Mackenzie gave me her usual sour look, the one that Angel said could fry the meat by itself.

I pulled Nanna's coat around me. "I was wondering…"

She said, "We can't give no charity today."

"I wasn't wanting none." Though if she'd handed me a link of those sausages, I wouldn't have said no.

"I just wondered why the sweet shop was closed."

"It's one of their religion days. None of 'em are around." She crossed her arms and glared at me. "If that's all you wanted, you'd best be going then."

I almost wished I was brave enough to grab the sausages and run off down the street with them, but Nanna had always been strict about not stealing. Other folks worked hard for what they had, she'd said. We had no right to take it. And anyway, people always remembered us.

I backed out, making sure I stared her in the eye. She looked away first.

The clock in Mrs Kastner's window said it was already past nine. I had to get money. But where from?

A greengrocer's cart was parked on the corner of Columbia Road and Hackney Road. *Anthony and Sons, Purveyors of Excellent Fruit and Veg. Top Quality.* The tailboard was down and Mr Anthony was weighing out carrots. Women were crowding around him, calling to be served next.

Fruit and veg. Of course. There's where I should have gone first!

I picked up my skirts and started running, Angel's boots squeezing my feet like claws.

Covent Garden Market. Nanna's family used to run a vegetable stall there. Her brother, my great-uncle Ned, would drop us round bags of potatoes and parsnips, but he'd packed up and moved out to Woodford just before Nanna died. He'd paid for her funeral, but he didn't want much to do with us. Nanna always said we didn't need anyone else. But we did. I did today.

I stood on the cobbled square outside the enormous market hall. It had taken me more than an hour to get there. My legs were wobbly from running and my breath felt like broken glass scraping up and down my throat. There were so many people, so many stalls, it was hard to know where to look. I tried to imagine pushing my way through, asking every single costermonger if they needed help.

I took one step, but all my strength had leaked out. I could smell the market — cabbages, hot pies from the barrow boys, horse dung from the trams and the cabs lined up in the side streets. I could hear the costermongers calling and the housekeepers and flower girls shouting for bargains. My feet still refused to move.

But I had to. I *had* to. My Angel was curled up

like a scrap of burnt paper in the corner of our bed. What if the spiders were creeping back? She hadn't eaten anything proper for more than a week. She didn't have enough strength to brush them away. And as soon as the clock chimed six, Bernard would come. It was so clear in my head. He'd climb the stairs, bend over the bed and sling my sister over his shoulder. Her hair would be draping down the back of his filthy waistcoat, her forehead bouncing against his shoulder as he stomped back down. He'd drop her in the gutter. I'd seen him do it to Mrs Astley, who used to be in the room above. Mrs Astley was kicking and punching at him every step of the way but it didn't make any difference. She'd still been left sitting on the street outside.

Nanna had pulled us away from the window to stop us looking.

And all I was doing now was standing there.

A cart rolled by. As I watched, a sack tipped and a cabbage thumped to the ground and rolled towards me. I hated cabbage but maybe I could trade it with Mrs Sweeting for some bread and maybe a little bit of bacon. I ran towards it, but as I bent down a small dirty hand scooped it up and hurtled away through the crowds.

What? No!

I spotted a flash of bare feet disappear behind the cart and round a corner. That cabbage was mine! I saw it first! I picked up my skirt and gave chase. But it was like everyone in Covent Garden was on the thief's side – the barrow boys, the housekeepers, the nannies, even the horses were against me. They closed round behind him, moved in front of me, wheeled their prams and barrows into me. I slumped against a pillar. I didn't have enough food in me to keep running. My sides felt like they'd been kicked by one of those carthorses. My breath sounded like it was whistling a tune. My breath? No, that wasn't me. Someone was blasting on a penny whistle. And I could hear a trumpet too.

The musicians were by the church railings. There were two girls. The one playing the trumpet was about my age. The younger one was blowing the penny whistle like an angry policeman. A small boy was sitting cross-legged at their feet, one arm waving the cap at passers-by, the other wrapped around a cabbage like it was his favourite toy. My cabbage.

A flower seller was slumped against the railings next to them, her bonnet drooped over her face, her basket of blooms wilting like she'd begged the broken ones from the stallholders and had tried to tie them together with string. There was a baby on her lap. It was wrapped in an old shawl, sucking its finger. For a second I thought of our little brother, still and silent in the bed beside Mama until Nanna wrapped him in a blanket and took him away.

The cabbage-thief glanced at me, then looked back, eyes wide. We stared at each other.

A woman stooped to drop a few coins in the cap. Suddenly the flower girl sprung to life as if there was a ghost behind the railings tugging her strings.

"Miss! Miss!" She held up some lily of the valley, the blossoms drooping like they were still asleep. "Miss!"

The woman glanced down, gave a little smile and walked on.

"Miss!" The flower girl was on her feet, the baby still in her arms as if it was glued there. She grabbed the basket of flowers. "Miss! Please buy some! They're half price! My baby's sick! Miss!"

The woman glanced back. She mouthed the words, "I'm sorry."

But I didn't care about her words. It was her face. It looked like mine. Not the way that Angel's was like mine. She couldn't be my sister. But her skin was light brown and she had dark, dark hair swept beneath a plain grey bonnet. For a moment our eyes met, then the flower seller caught up with her. And she was hurrying off, the flower girl keeping pace by her side.

A woman. Who looked like me. A woman in clean clothes that fit her properly, who wasn't pushing strangers' washing around a metal tub. She wasn't sweeping sawdust around the table legs and chair backs or walking backwards out of the butcher's shop because she didn't want to feel the shame burning into her back. A woman. Who looked like me.

I breathed in. I felt like my tiredness had been swept away with the swish of her skirt. A horse clopped by, its cart full of bulging sacks of vegetables. A porter strode past, a stack of flower boxes balanced on his head. There was laughter behind me. A little boy and his sister were playing hide and seek in the cemetery. My pockets were still empty, but they didn't have to be.

I walked over to the musicians. The child's eyes widened and he grabbed the cabbage so hard it jerked out of his hands and rolled across the cobbles. He lunged for it, but I got there first. I picked it up. The trumpet player stopped.

"Don't you go near him!"

I dropped the cabbage back in his lap. "I wasn't going to."

"Well, clear off then."

"I want to sing with you."

"You what?"

"I can sing!"

The girl with the whistle scowled. "You can't." She turned to the trumpet player. "She can't, can she, Enid?"

Enid shook her head. "We're not splitting four ways."

I glanced at the empty cap. "You can't split nothing four ways. Just let me try."

Before they could say anything else, I took a deep breath in, opened my mouth and let my voice curl round the tune. *All Things Bright and Beautiful.*

✱

Ding! It was five o'clock! Dong! But Enid wanted me to stay for one more tune. Ding! I had to get home for Angel! Dong! The cap was heavy with coins but the posh opera folk would make it heavier. Ding! But Bernard... Dong! Bernard.

I promised Enid I'd be back the next day, shoved my share of money in my pockets and ran.

The clock at Liverpool Street Station said five to six. My heart felt like it was going to jump out of my mouth and run down the road by itself. I hurled myself through our front door, pulled myself up the stairs and stopped. A blanket had been nailed across the door space. And there were voices coming from the other side.

I slid down the wall on to the dirty floor. Bernard had done it. He'd thrown Angel out on to the street and given our room to someone else.

"When Victoria comes…"

I sat up straight. *Victoria*. Did they mean me? No, I knew about five other Victorias. But the voice – that sounded like Angel. Not the tough, loud Angel I knew before, but definitely *Angel!*

I forced myself to stand up. I pushed the blanket aside. My sister was sitting at the table with a bowl of steaming soup in front of her. Soup?

A woman I'd never seen before was sitting next to her. She turned to look at me. Her face was kind and open. A man was standing by the fireplace. He was short and thin. It looked like his jacket could go round him twice. He was frowning.

I ran to my sister, the coins knocking together in my pocket.

She smiled. "I told them you'd come, Vicky."

She picked up a spoonful of soup and offered it to me. I shook my head and it sloshed back into the bowl, the spoon clanking against the enamel.

"I tried to get her to eat." The woman put an arm round Angel's shoulder. "You have to eat, love."

"My soup," the man muttered. "That's my good soup the girl's got."

The woman twisted round and glared at him. "Stop it, George. You've had yours already and there's more in the pot."

"Even so, Lou. She's taking food right out of our own children's mouths."

The dirt-smeared windows let in so little light, I hadn't noticed the children huddled on our bed. Two of them must have been twins, with another smaller one between them. None of them could have been more than five.

Footsteps. Workboots slamming down on wooden stairs. Lou shoved herself away from the table and went and crouched by her children, arms around them. Her husband, George, turned towards the cold fireplace.

72

Angel opened her mouth. "Bernard."

"It's all right," I whispered. "I have the money."

The blanket was yanked from the doorframe, threads left dangling down from the nails. A pale fist, knuckles cracking. Angel huddled against me.

I took her hand. Her fingers were as light as a ghost's. I couldn't see Bernard's face, but I could smell him. Blood and smoke and street dirt.

Lou's voice from the corner. "You've no right to come in here. We've paid. Tell him, George!"

George didn't turn round.

In the room above, I could hear Mrs Sweeting dragging her tub across the floor. Her baby was crying. One of Lou's children whimpered.

Lou's voice had shrunk, but I heard her. "George? Please."

George clutched his jacket around himself, then turned to face us. "We paid you a week upfront, Mr Vickery."

Bernard snorted. "You paid for your family. Not for these two. That's extra."

I said, "I have money."

I dug in my pocket, pulled out the coins and held them in my palm. Three heavy footsteps. My head filled up with Bernard's stink. I could hear Angel's breath, in and out, quick, like she wanted to speak but had lost her words. I closed my eyes. The coins were swept from my hand and the footsteps headed away. They stopped.

"You've bought one more night."

My eyes snapped open. "Another night? That's enough for a week!"

A laugh from the staircase. "Didn't your new friends tell you? Rent's gone up."

George rubbed his eyes with the back of his hand. "It seems like we're stuck with you."

"George!" Lou stood up, hands on her hips. "That's uncharitable. And they paid, you saw them!"

"None of that money's going into our pockets, Lou. Are they getting breakfast on the house too?"

"Stop!" Lou stepped towards him. The twin was crying louder now, sobs that made the heavy air shake.

I stood up. "He's right. You're under no obligation to us."

Angel's fingers scrabbled against my shoulder. "Let me go to Mama. Please."

I kissed her cheek. My lips were damp from her crying. "No, Angelica. You have to stay here. Lou?

Please can you look after my sister?"

"No," Angel said. "Just let me go."

"Lou," I said. "Can you?"

Lou nodded. "But you don't have to go."

But I did. Other than our globe and Nanna's bonnet, Angel and I had nothing left in the world. Even if we had somewhere to stay tonight, what would happen tomorrow?

✦

London night. Light and shadows. The moon was hidden behind the clouds. The street lamps had been lit, but voices called from dark corners. This time I was lucky. I crept on to an omnibus at Old Street and the conductor let me stay.

Covent Garden Market was closed but it still felt like the whole of London was there. Ladies in fur jackets and heavy, sweeping skirts strolled arm in arm with gentlemen. Flower girls sat by every lamppost calling out their wares, their baskets of blooms by their sides. A barrow boy pushed past me yelling out, "Fried eels." My stomach tightened.

Enid, please still be here! I weaved my way through the crowd towards the church. *Please, Enid! Please!*

But an organ grinder had taken their place. He had a little monkey on a leash dressed in a tiny jacket and trilby. He was pulling on the leash trying to make the monkey dance, but it was fighting to get away.

"Sir!" A woman bent over the monkey, trying to untangle the lead from around its neck. "This is needless cruelty."

The monkey shot forward, teeth bared. The woman jumped back.

The organ grinder smirked. "It's a cruel beast, madam."

The woman straightened up. It was her! The one who'd walked off across the square with the flower girl pleading at her heels. The one with skin the same colour as mine.

"A cruel beast indeed," she said. "But I'm not talking about the monkey."

She managed to unloop the lead and headed away. I ran after her.

"Miss!" Her dark-blue dress wove between the opera suits and lush silks and velvets. "Miss!"

I hadn't noticed the puddle of water and wet leaves. A flower girl must have emptied out her bucket. I slipped and flew forward, grabbing a handful of the woman's jacket.

She spun round. "Thief!"

"No! I'm not a thief!" I glanced around, in case a policeman had heard her. Luckily I didn't see any. I let the soft fabric fall through my fingers. "I just … I just need to talk to you."

Her face softened. "Have we met before?"

She remembered me! "This afternoon. Right here, by the musicians."

"Oh, yes." She sighed. "Are you here by yourself? You look so young. What do you want from me?"

"I … I want…" But what did I want? She didn't look rich. What could she do for us? "It's just me and my sister. We've got nowhere to go. Angel's been sick since our grandma died and we're going to end up in the workhouse."

She gave me a little smile. "Is that so bad?"

My breath stopped. Didn't she know? DIDN'T SHE KNOW? I swung round and walked away. I felt a hand on my shoulder.

"Sorry. I'm not from London. I don't always understand. Is the workhouse really so bad? I don't know. I've never had the misfortune to have to enter one."

Her eyes were shaded by her broad hat. Her face was hard to read.

"Yes," I said. "It is. They don't really want to

help us so they make it as bad as possible. Me and Angel, we'd be split up. I'm strong, but Angel – she isn't. I don't know what to do."

"I don't know what I can do. I have so little money."

"Mrs Vickery's our landlady. Her son, Bernard, took all my money. Maybe you can talk to her."

"I don't know. Why me?"

I touched her hand, the same light brown as me and Angel, then touched mine. "Please?"

"I'll try," she said. "That's all I can promise. What's your name?"

"I'm Victoria."

"Hello, Victoria. I'm Miss Malvery. Olive Malvery."

✱

We took a cab back east. Miss Malvery bought some bread, hot pies and apples to bring with us. The driver dropped us by Liverpool Street Station and Miss Malvery followed me through the dark narrow streets to our home.

I pushed open the front door but Miss Malvery let it swing shut. We were in darkness. She breathed in sharply. I reached behind and offered her my hand. She took it, holding it tight. I knew every groan and dip of those rotting steps.

The blanket had been nailed back over the door. I pulled it aside. George stepped forward towards us.

He glanced at Miss Malvery, then at me.

"She's gone," he said.

Gone? Who?

I looked round the room. Lou was sitting on a stool by a small fire. The children were top-and-toe in bed. The table had been cleared. Angel's chair was empty. My heart felt like it was punching itself.

"Where is she?"

Lou half rose. "We tried to stop her, Victoria. We really did."

"Did she say where she was going?"

Lou and George swapped a look.

"To find your mother," Lou said.

Each beat of my heart, a thud of pain.

"Is your mother far away?" Miss Malvery asked.

I tried to say the words but my mouth felt too heavy to move.

She was still holding my hand. She squeezed it. "Would you like me to come with you?"

I nodded.

There weren't so many street lights near our

home. The gas lighters didn't like coming here in case they got robbed. But the public houses were well lit and candles flickered in the windows of the houses. We passed the men queuing for the lodging house and the old women dressed in tattered black who always sat on the benches in Itchy Park. Miss Malvery wanted to know where they slept. I knew that some of them lived in the broken-down sheds crammed between the privies in the back yards. Others slept on the benches in the day and walked the street at night. We walked past the building where Mama used to work. There was just one small window in that room where she and five others made artificial flowers for rich ladies' hats. She had to work quickly as she was only paid for each flower. But each one had to be perfect or else she wouldn't get any money for it. She'd been sent away when the gossip reached the supervisor that Mama was expecting a child. That was my poor little brother who never opened his eyes.

I was the first to see Angel, on the corner of Vallance Road and Fournier Street, leaning against Whitechapel Union Infirmary wall. She was wearing Nanna's bonnet. It was light grey in the gloom, but on bright days the colours seemed to glow, especially the blue flowers Mama made specially to decorate it.

I ran up to Angel and wrapped her in my arms. She was only wearing a thin dress.

"Here." Miss Malvery draped her own shawl around Angel's shoulders. I pulled it tight and pinned it in place.

"Angel?" I didn't want to say the words that were bubbling up through me. "Mama's not here any more. Nanna told us. Do you remember?"

The shawl hadn't made much difference. Angel was shivering so hard I thought she'd fall apart.

"We need to get her into the warmth," Miss Malvery said. "Would you like some hot chocolate, Angelica?"

"Our brother died." Angel's voice almost faded into the night. "Mama said she still saw him when she was sleeping. He'd be alive and smiling at her. She said she just wanted to carry on sleeping. She wouldn't..."

"She wouldn't eat or drink," I said. "She wouldn't talk to us."

She'd just lain in bed with her face turned to the wall, her cheeks powdery from the dried tears. In the end, Nanna had brought her here hoping the doctors could help her. She'd died two weeks later.

"Sorry," Angel whispered. "I should be helping you, but sometimes everything seems so hard. If I wasn't around, it would be easier for you."

"How can you say that? You're my sister! I love you more than the world."

Suddenly her arms were around me too, her face in my hair, like the times we used to snuggle up under the blankets while Mama sang to us.

Miss Malvery's arms circled both of us. "I'm sorry too." She held us closer. "So sorry that you were left alone and had nowhere to go. I've rented a room in Covent Garden, next to Enid and her family. Though it's not much better than your home now."

There'd be no Bernard. And we'd have Miss Malvery.

"If you stay with me tonight," she said, "we can try and find you somewhere more suitable tomorrow."

I whispered, "What do you think, Angel?"

"Yes," she said. "Please."

"Good." Miss Malvery steered us away from the infirmary. "Enid said you sing well, Victoria. I'm a music teacher. Did you know that?"

"No, Miss Malvery."

She sighed. "There's no reason why you should know." She wiped her eyes. "There are so many things that I don't know too." She glanced back at the infirmary. "But I think that now is the time for me to find out."

Olive Christian Malvery (1877–1914) was born in Lahore, now in Pakistan. Her parents were English and Indian. She came to London when she was twenty-three and was shocked by the way poorer women were treated. She made friends with the women, living in the same run-down rooms, working in the same jobs as them and pretending to be homeless so she could experience the workhouse conditions. She wrote about the experience in magazines and books, and campaigned on behalf of the women all her life. When she married, she invited costermongers from Hoxton to be her bridesmaids and a thousand working women as her guests.

THE
GREEN-
HEARTED
GIRL

KIRAN
MILLWOOD HARGRAVE

Once, there was a weather witch whose heart broke. She loved someone, and they died. First she cried, so long and so hard that the clouds pitied her and cried with her. Together they churned the land to mud and swelled the streams to rivers, the lakes to oceans. Towns were washed away; cities sank underwater. The witch had not meant to cause the destruction, and it broke her heart to have harmed so many. Her own dying wish was that one day a green-hearted child would be born who would undo the harm she had done.

When her heart broke, it split into seven pieces, and from each piece grew a tree of a different sort: an apple tree, an oak, a birch, an ash, a walnut, a cedar and a willow. The trees took root in mud at the base of the great churning ocean of tears, spending their sapling years waving thinly as coral beneath the water. The salt, which would normally kill trees, made these seven grow strong and shining as crystal, with leaves as wide as sails. Though the ocean was very deep, the trees grew taller and taller every day, until at last they reached the surface.

When they emerged at the seven corners of the ocean, those people who had survived the flood sighted them. When they reached them, they each believed their tree to be the best, though the trees had more in common than was different.

In time, the people made streets of their boughs and beds of their blossom. They wove great nets from shredded twigs and caught shoals of tuna and swordfish. A few of the people had pocketfuls of dirt and seeds from their gardens – whatever they had saved before they were washed away. In the lowermost branches they grew mushrooms and other things that fed on the dark. At the top they made skygardens, carving hollow troughs in the tree with swordfish swords and planting seeds of lettuce and rhubarb, cabbage and asparagus.

The walnut tree grew walnuts as big as double beds that fed whole families for a week, and the cases could be waterproofed with wax from the bees that nested in the uppermost branches and made into nutcase boats with leaf sails. The apple tree-dwellers had smoked apples, with pips as dark and shiny as beetle eyes, which they split open to collect the poison for arrows, to catch the larger prey of the ocean. The birch and ash towns had ornate staircases weaving from branch to branch like wooden spiders' webs. The cedar smelled so beautiful when burned that other treeple – as they came to call themselves – came from all around. The oak tree was the favourite of owls, and the inhabitants used their hoots like clocks. And those who lived in the willow wove great baskets to catch the rain and to sleep in.

Occasionally they traded, sailing in their basket boats or walnut cases to swap acorns for honey, cider for willow rope. Soil was valued above all: with soil, they could plant more food, and grow herbs and medicine. So much rain made people sick, even if they were kept dry beneath the canopies of leaves. The damp seeped under their skin, shrivelling them like raisins. Their lungs grew saltmould; their armpits lichen. But over time, they adapted.

And so did their history. At first there were still people who had once lived in towns and cities. They told their children about dry land, dirt and sand beneath their toes and the feeling of sun on their faces, lives lived on the horizontal rather than the vertical. But eventually these became myths, less and less remembered, less and less real. But all remembered the witch, and as one generation passed the stories on to the next, she grew monstrous and cruel, sending the rain on purpose.

The origin of the trees was forgotten, her final sacrifice changed into the story of her slaying by a group of determined humans, known as seedkings, who were clever enough to plant the trees before they were flooded.

The clouds wept to see her slandered, and the rain grew harder and more wicked. By the seventieth generation, one thousand and four hundred years since the witch's heart broke, the children had known only rain. Every sproutday, a new ring was drawn about their heart, so they could mark their growth the same way trees do. Their arms were long and strong for climbing, their skin thick against splinters. Their hair was thick, thatched with salt, their lashes long to keep out rain. The apple-tree children had small teeth, softened by eating so much sugar: those from the walnut towns could crack the hard cases between enamel slabs as strong as rock.

They spoke the same language as their parents, but for different purposes. No one talked about the weather, because the weather was always the same. The oak-dwellers worshipped owls, the cedar treeple had cedar-incense celebrations every quarter cloud, when the sea rose three clean feet, pulled by the unseen moon.

But while they each developed their own culture and customs, none of them could fail to notice that the trees were not growing as fast as the ocean was rising. Where once there had been five thousand feet of tree above the waterline, now there were three thousand. The more the treeple flourished, the less the space. Within another ten generations, they would have to abandon the trees.

This thought made the treeple afraid, and afraid people are often the most dangerous. They began blaming their neighbouring trees for the rising seas. A war, brief as a squall, broke out between oak and birch over fishing rights to the stretch of sea between them. Apple negotiated a peace, but the damage was done. Each of the trees stopped trading with each other, and the treelands descended into uneasy isolation at the seven corners of their shared ocean.

But the clouds remembered the witch's promise, that one day a child would come along who would undo the harm the witch had unwittingly caused. And when the child was born, it was the clouds who recognised her. They knitted themselves tight as brows, drew darkness into their furrows and murmured in their low, rolling language, bringing evermore rain. And as droplets tapped their tentative warning through the trailing tendrils of the willow, the green-hearted girl took her first breath.

✶

Alba Salix was a tiny thing, whippet thin and slightly green, like new wood. The clouds seemed to crowd lower over her woven crib, peering in and flashing their lightning grins as the chief midwife gave Alba a dot over her heart, around which all future rings would be drawn. Alba wailed, and the clouds wailed back as the midwives drew the leaf-wick curtains closed.

"A sickly podling," muttered one midwife to another. "Must have some ash sap in her."

"She may yet sprout," chided the other. "Give her a quarter cloud."

And sprout she did. Like all podlings, she was raised by the whole family tree, with many mothers and many fathers. Alba grew no wider, staying crown-thin as a pruned branch, but she was long as a root by her fifth sproutday, towering over her seedmates. The chief midwife did not even have to bend to draw the fifth ring around her heart.

Over time, the greenish tinge retreated to her hair, eyebrows and eyelashes, and though she suffered the usual ailments growing up – crop-croup, callus-colic, root-rythmia – she was otherwise healthy. Except…

Except there was a seed-small part of her heart that felt wrong. To begin with she hardly noticed it, other than as a shadow under each heartbeat, but as she learned more about the seven-cornered ocean and the treelands, about the evil witch and the good seedkings, the wrongness grew. By her eleventh sproutday, it felt so wrong she fancied that when she knocked her long-fingered fist on her chest it was as hollow as a dead trunk, as brittle as an abandoned bird's nest.

If it had just been this feeling inside her, she might have been able to ignore it, because we are very good at ignoring ourselves, though we shouldn't. It took other people saying something was wrong for her to believe it. And others said so, all the time, because just as they had on the first day of her life, the clouds followed her. Just wisps to begin with, indiscernible from breath on a cold day. But year on year, the wisps increased, catching behind her ears and between her toes. As her hollowness increased, so did the clouds.

When Alba reached school-going age, her seedmates insisted on a wax-proofed curtain between them and Alba, because the clouds drew themselves so close to her she was near-constantly enveloped, making her and those around her as damp as the lettuces in the skygarden.

"It's because you're so miserable," her seedmates would tease. "You cry so much, the clouds think you're one of them."

They didn't stop to consider that perhaps it was their teasing that made Alba cry. In fact, Alba rather liked the clouds: it was as if they had chosen her as special to them.

Still, it was a definite inconvenience to constantly live in the damp even when she was inside. Her clothes rotted at the seams, her hair was more frizz than strand. The cloud-coming was especially bad when they studied Wistory: the history of the willow and how it was the first tree planted – though all the treeple claimed theirs was – and, of course, how the rain began. It was already a tricky concept for the pod to grasp: that rain was something that "began" and so perhaps used to "stop", and some of Alba's pod questioned the need to be taught it at all.

"It happened so long ago," they moaned, which was, in essence, the definition of Wistory. "Who cares?"

But Alba cared. She was fascinated by the idea that people had once lived differently, that the ocean had a bottom, and that the sky went on above the clouds. And most of all, she was fascinated by the witch. Whenever the witch was mentioned, Alba felt the hollow in her chest fill a little, and the clouds seemed to swarm around her, making low sounds that could have been whispers if she did not know it was impossible for them to talk.

Except it wasn't. Clouds talked all the time: rain was one of their languages. They also spoke in thunder and lightning. Sometimes they played charades, so well that before the rain, people cloudgazing could point and say "train" or "sheep". But very few people could understand them, only weather witches. So Alba could not know what they were trying to say, until the night of her twelfth sproutday.

She always slept apart from the rest of her pod, close to the skygarden in a high-sided woven basket, unwaxed because there was no point in waterproofing it: the clouds seeped in to settle beside her anyway. Lately the clouds had got so thick about her she found that if she lay rigid and wafted her arms in and out, like she was floating, she could guide enough cloud beneath her to almost hover.

She pulled some of it across her eyes to soothe the slight headache that had been building all day. Alba never looked forward to her sproutday: while it was marked with the ring-giving, none of her seedmates came to watch.

"You will though, won't you?" said Alba to the clouds. She felt a damp coolness press against her ear, like a wet kiss.

Yes.

Alba froze. It was perhaps not quite right that she'd heard the word "yes". There was no sound like "y" or "e", and only a slight "s" like the lifting of steam. But Alba understood that it meant "yes", sure as a nod.

"Did ... did you say something?" Alba did not feel silly speaking to the clouds. She always had. It was only that they had never spoken back before.

Yes.

Something swelled in her chest like she had never

felt before. Alba felt tears prick at her eyelids and slide down her cheeks, only discernable from rain by their warmth. The clouds sent more water to chase them away, and it felt gentle as a fingertip.

Sorry it took so long to talk to you. We had to wait for you to be older, to be sure you were ready.

"Ready?" Alba wiped her face dry; more rain dampened it almost instantly, dripping off her long green lashes. "Ready for what?"

To fix the witch's heart.

The warmth of her joy melted. This was definitely a dream.

"All right," she said, louder this time. "Wake up now."

We're awake.

"Not you, me!" Alba pinched the back of her left hand.

She's confused. The cloud spoke in one voice, but as though it were many.

Alba squeezed her eyes shut. "Dreaming. I'm dreaming."

When Alba opened her eyes again, the clouds had grouped close to her head, like a concerned pod over a sick child.

You're the green-hearted child she said would come.

"Green-hearted?"

Good, kind, strong, but still bendable enough to believe. Green.

"I'm not strong." Alba flexed her sapling-thin arm to show the cloud. "See?"

Green, though. A wisp traced her eyebrows, flowed through her hair. *We saw you when you were born. Your heart glowed green right through you. You are the one the witch said would come.*

"The witch? The evil witch who caused all this?"

The clouds darkened. Its voice was thundery, rattling Alba's mind. *She meant no harm. She was young and too powerful. She could not undo what she did in her lifetime. But she made the trees, and she made you.*

"I'm not witch-made!" said Alba, startled. "And the treelands were planted by the seedkings."

The clouds rumbled a laugh that blew cold wind up Alba's nose. *She is the trees.*

Alba had had enough. She wanted to wake up now. Before she could think better of it she rolled sharply to her left, over and out of her bed basket.

Instantly she realised her mistake. She was not waking up – she was still falling. Her stomach was left behind as she plummeted, the long tendrils of the willow whipping past her. She looked up to the rain-sodden sky, knowing that below her the swirling sea was rushing up to meet her—

And then the clouds were plunging in a great wave, scooping underneath her back and flooding between her grabbing fingers. Thinner, wind-whipped wisps grasped at her hair while more and more cloud funnelled down from the sky until she stopped completely. Then, they began to lift her.

Now *do you believe you're awake?*

Alba could only gasp and nod.

Then let us tell you about the witch.

She was flying. They lifted her to the uppermost boughs of the willow and carried her in a slow, drifting circle. The rain fell lightly and soft, like feathers, as the cloud spoke of a good but broken-hearted witch who cried Alba's world into being, and who promised the world a chance to return to how it was.

And here you are. Just in time, too. The ocean rises yearly.

"Can't you just stop raining?"

We can no more stop raining than you can stop breathing. She holds us here; her sorrow keeps us.

"Why me? What can I do?"

You can fix her heart.

"How?"

You need to go to the other trees and tell them the truth. To fix her heart, you must make them remember.

Alba finally understood. She had to change people's minds about the witch. More than that, she had to change their hearts.

Alba sat carefully up on the cloud. "All right. Where first?"

Ash is closest. The cloud seemed to shimmer with gladness. *Hold on.*

✸

Cloud flying was the scariest thing Alba had ever known. It was not the height – no treeple were scared of heights – but the speed. It peeled back her lips from her teeth and her eyelids from her eyes and made whiplashes of the rain. They went so fast the cloud tore itself to pieces and was constantly having to re-form beneath her. It would dissolve under her hands like applefloss and she would begin a slow-motion plummet until it reassembled thickly enough to support her again.

But cloud flying was also the most startlingly wonderful thing Alba had ever known. The clouds carried her so high she fancied she could almost see their end and the moon beyond. She saw the great far-off masts of the other treelands, spiking along the horizon like points on an uneven sundial.

They reached Ash three raincycles after Alba's twelfth sproutday. The cloud deposited her gently on the midbough, and Alba's legs had forgotten how to stand. She collapsed forward through a thick wall of leaves, face-first into an Ash-woman's seedsoup.

"Great Mulch!" cried a woman's voice. When Alba blinked up at her, green eyelashes dripping, she saw that she looked like Willowfolk, not monstrous as her teachers taught them. Only their clothes were different: Alba's were woven, but the Ash-woman's were a series of interlocking discs of wafer-thin wood.

"Where in rain's name did you come from?" said the woman, recovering herself and helping Alba to her unsteady feet.

"Willow," said Alba, concentrating on standing upright.

"How on tree did you get here?" said the woman, parting the thick wall of leaves and peering out. The clouds seeped in through the gap and swirled into Alba's ears.

Tell her the truth.

So Alba did. "The clouds brought me."

The woman blinked slowly, and then smiled a smile that did not reach her eyes. "Did you fall, dear? Did you bang your head?"

"No, they really did!" said Alba, about to go on when the clouds in her ears said *No. She's not the heart. Find someone who believes.*

Alba steadied herself just in time, turning to look back at the Ash-woman. She looked back with suspicious eyes, as though Alba was dangerous. She knew what the clouds meant: the woman did not seem the sort of person who would believe in the witch's tale.

"You're right," said Alba. "Sorry, just a little dazed." She edged past the woman.

She felt the woman's eyes on her until she reached the trunk and, not seeing that she had a choice, began climbing. The ash's branches were spaced a lot further apart than the willow's, but with Alba's long arms it wasn't too much of a problem. She climbed and climbed until she reached the top of the ash. To her great surprise she found a skygarden there, though the Willowfolk were taught from podlings that they were a Willow invention. She plucked a small lettuce leaf from the nearest plot and was just about to munch it down when something landed in her lap.

A seed, said the clouds. *An ash seed.*

"But how did it fall up?" asked Alba.

"I threw it," said a voice, and Alba jumped, nearly losing her grip on the branch below. She spun round and saw a boy sitting nearby. It was obvious why she had not noticed him before. His dark-brown hair was strewn with leaves and his face streaked with precious dirt. He looked like an extension of the tree itself.

Before she could say anything else, he threw another of the seeds upwards, and Alba watched as it danced down, spinning in a tight circle. "Haven't you ever seen a seed before?"

"Not an ash one," said Alba. "I'm from Willow."

"Really?" said the boy. "Thought I hadn't seen you around before. But you're *not* ugly—" He broke off and blushed. "I mean. You're not *not* ugly. You're not anything that I noticed, but my teachers said you're all warty and snarly and weeping."

"And my teachers said you're all two feet tall with sharp grey teeth. I think they might have lied to us."

"Unless you're lying." He frowned at her and cocked his head, sending a few leaves tumbling from his hair. "How did you get here?"

Alba took a deep breath, feeling her heart knocking its hollow drum against her chest. "The clouds brought me."

The boy frowned at her. But then he looked behind her, at the cluster of clouds, and nodded. "All right. What's your name?"

Relief flooded her as the clouds sang in her ears. *He's the one!* "Alba. What's yours?"

"Ask. Why'd you come here?"

And Alba told him about the clouds speaking to her, and the truth of the treelands, and the witch's broken heart. Ask listened silently, the dark-brown pools of his eyes widening.

"And so I need you to come with me," finished Alba breathlessly. "To the other trees. And when we have one person from each, the witch's heart will be mended and the oceans will stop rising."

"How?" said Ask, and while Alba was relieved he had questioned none of her tale, her relief faded when she realised she didn't have the answer.

"How?" she asked the clouds.

You'll know, green-hearted girl.

"You can't expect me to come with you if you don't know how to fix it," said Ask fairly. "What would be the point?"

Alba was saved from making up an answer by a squawk from the lower branches. "There! There's the Willow-spy!"

She felt a tug on her leg as, through the leaves, came the woman whose soup she'd spilled, together with several other Ashfolk, one of whom had her leg in a vice-like grip. She wrenched herself free and backed away to the end of the branch.

"I'm no spy," she said. "Leave me alone!"

But the Ashfolk advanced, and Alba knew she was out of time. The clouds rushed forwards in a sharp blast of icy air, and the Ashfolk paused just long enough for Alba to lock eyes with the Ash-boy.

"Come with me!" she cried, and threw herself backwards. The clouds hurried to catch her, and a moment later she felt a thump beside her. The people above were leaning over the branches, gesticulating wildly. She turned to see Ask, face pale at his own bravery, lying in the white beside her.

"This... is..." He trailed off.

Alba grinned. "Hold on."

Oak, here we come, murmured the cloud, and bore

them away.

✳

Alba had learned her lesson – no more grown-ups. She was beginning to understand what green-hearted meant: while the children they collected did not actually have green hearts or hair, they were exactly as a tree was when it was first planted – strong though it was small, adaptable to weather and weeds and doubt. On Oak they found a girl called Querc with no voice and an open heart. On Birch there were twins, Silver and Sylvia, who were expert liars and believed difficult truths better than easy ones. On Cedar they found a boy named Ceylon, who believed in his heart straightaway, but whose head took some convincing.

Every day the sea rose a little higher. It was a dozen raincycles since Alba had left – she was halfway to her thirteenth sproutday – and the water was swallowing the mushroom field on Willow. And now there was danger of a different sort: after Alba's escape with Ask, envoys from the ash tree were sent to warn the other trees about her.

"A Willow-spy has taken one of our own. We saw her spirit him away in a flying willoweave basket." For this is what they thought the clouds were. "We come to warn you, and to ask for your aid in recovering our lost sapling."

Soon the message spread that other saplings were missing from other trees. The residents of Apple and Walnut went on high alert, keeping their saplings cupped into the centremost points of the trees. The clouds saw the preparations and passed along the message to Alba.

"How will we get in?" said Alba, explaining to the others. But Silver and Sylvia only smiled and said in unison, "Let us go."

So a plan was formed: the clouds increased their downpour over Walnut until everyone, saplings included, retreated to the lower branches. They drifted Silver and Sylvia in on a separate little cloud during the confusion of the storm, and the twins lied their way down the tree until they fell in with the drenched saplings. Once there, they did what they had never done before: told the truth. Soon the cloud that carried them was zooming back with an extra passenger, a girl called Fen who had always wanted to leave her treeland and meet other treeple.

They had been lucky thus far, but as they closed in on Apple, the treeple had developed a way of communicating with smoke and fire, and knew what to look out for. As the group of saplings approached, they readied themselves. An Applechild named Pip saw the preparations and, never one to ignore a fuss, concealed himself nearby.

When Alba saw the wide branch at the top of Apple, cleared of leaves and spiky twigs, and seeming perfect for landing a cloud, she knew something was wrong, especially after the difficulty at Walnut.

"It looks like a trap," she said, scanning the surrounding boughs. "Perhaps we should wait a while."

"Don't be silly," said Ask. "Take good luck where you find it."

"What do you think?" Alba asked the clouds, but they were distracted by the vessels crossing the ocean and had not seen what lay in wait. *We are too close to turn back now.*

But as soon as the children alighted on the landing branch, the ground beneath them turned into the bodies and grabbing hands of the Apple Corps. The cloudmates were no match for the highly trained soldiers in their uniforms of bark, and though the clouds raged and made fog of everything, Alba could only struggle helplessly as a hand clapped a cloth coated in a sleeping poison over her mouth.

A smaller hand grabbed at her, and Alba looked down to see an Applechild trying to free her. Pip grappled with the Apple Corps soldier with all his tiny might, but the man swatted him aside and another soldier picked him up. Not recognising he was an Applechild, the soldier drugged him too. Alba felt her lungs burn for a moment, and then she fell into a deep, dark sleep.

When she awoke she felt thirstier than she ever had in her life. The ground seemed to rise and fall beneath her feet, just as it did on the cloud, but it felt solid, like wood. The clouds rushed forwards anxiously and coated her dry tongue, as Alba looked down to see bark shackles on her wrists and feet.

"Clear, please," she asked the clouds, and when they parted she saw her cloudmates similarly tied at points around a vessel of pale applewood. The Applechild who had tried to help her was there too. Two Apple Corps soldiers stood keeping watch as others rowed. Alba gasped. They were on the ocean.

"Where are you taking us?" she said, and a sour-faced soldier turned towards her. In his hand he held a knotted whip formed of apple stems.

"Back where you came from," he sneered. "We're returning all of you to your treelands. And when we get to Willow, we will punish the Willowfolk for your crimes."

"Tell 'em, Smith," crowed another soldier.

Alba felt her body fill with sorrow. She had failed, and her home would be punished for it.

"What crimes?" said Silver and Sylvia.

"Kidnap and lies. We know you've been telling tales about the witch. That one told us your ridiculous tale about hearts and crying."

Smith gestured to Fen, who was crumpled in her shackles. Alba's sadness turned to anger. What had they done to her?

"She's been telling the truth," said Ask desperately. "We weren't kidnapped, we followed her!"

"Do you need to be punished also?" Smith took a threatening step towards her friend, raising his whip as if to strike.

"No!" Now Alba's anger grew. She felt it from the tips of her toes to the ends of her hair. She looked down and saw her skin was glowing green, and her chest felt as hot as fire. Suddenly a spike of lightning thrust down and struck, right next to the sour-faced soldier.

"What the—" he yelled, and reared back. There was a small smoking hole beside him. The rest of the Apple Corps rose to their feet, abandoning their oars.

Alba looked at her hands, her feet, placed her shackled hand over her frantically beating heart. "I didn't... I didn't mean to—"

But Smith lifted her roughly to her feet. "What trick was that," he asked. "Are there more Willow-spies about?"

But Alba finally understood what she was, and what to do. "No, it was me." She pulled her arm free. "I'm a weather witch."

The clouds rumbled their joy. *You are, you are!*

Smith spat on the ground by her feet. "You're a mad girl and I'm not wasting my time on you. You're stinking spies, all of you." He reeled round. "Throw them over!"

Alba felt a desperate, wrenching force rip through her as the Apple Corps surrounded her cloudmates. Her shackles fell away like smoke and she gasped. It was as if the clouds held their breath with her, and as she exhaled they rushed down so fast it was as if the sky was falling. High above, more clouds rained and thundered, and the ocean rose and rose. On the treelands, the treeple rushed for the uppermost branches.

The vessel was thrown this way and that, but the clouds kept Alba upright as she leaned over Smith, who clung to the mast, illuminated by her ghostly green light. She bent down low over him and said in a voice like rain, "Now do you believe me?"

It didn't matter if Smith did or did not. Because Pip the Applechild had heard her story, seen the storm be conjured, and he raised his piping voice high above the thunder of the sky and sea and said joyfully, fearfully, "Yes!"

The moment he said this, the rain stopped. Not just lightened, but stopped. The silence was so sudden and so complete it felt deafening. No one living had ever heard the sound of no rain.

And then, somewhere deep below the vessel, where the tree roots reached for miles across the seabed towards each other and intertwined, a chasm opened. The vessel was caught in a great swirling whirlpool that began to suck the water away.

"What's happening?" cried Alba. *You did it*, said the clouds. *You fixed her heart. You* are *her heart.*

Alba clung to Ask, who clung to Silver, who clung to Pip, who clung to Sylvia, and on and on as they were thrown this way and that, until finally something caught them and lifted them clear of the draining ocean. The clouds came and carried the children down to the ground.

Alba felt the clouds clearing and tried desperately to hold them close to her. *Don't worry*, they said. *We'll be back to fill the lakes.*

"But what will I do without you? I don't want to be alone."

Ask heard her words, saw her eyes filling with tears and the disappearing clouds, and guessed they were going away. He slipped his hand into hers. "You won't be alone."

At the seven corners of the fading ocean, the treelanders watched until all that was left of the sea were two great lakes. Far-off cities gleamed in the newly revealed sunshine. From all of it rose a steam, lifting like a tide.

For the first time in their lives, the treeple climbed down from the trees and walked across the once-oceanbed from the seven corners of their world. They met in the middle, blinking and sunburned, where an undrowned city waited. And caught on the highest building was an applewood vessel with Apple Corps soldiers calling down to be rescued.

Nearby was a small knot of children, one from each tree, all tangled up as tree roots in a hug. And at the centre was a green-hearted girl, mourning for the clouds. She didn't cry though; she knew better than to start that again.

TEA
AND
JAM

KATHERINE
WOODFINE

The cloth spread on the tray. The milk in the jug. The cups on the saucers.

A heap of snow-white sugar cubes in the basin. Beside them, the silver tongs – designed for lifting a single cube delicately, because a lady doesn't shovel in a heaping spoon of sugar, not like in the kitchen at home. Butter in a little dish, and scones on a plate – but not too many, because that wouldn't be ladylike either. It feels like forever since dinnertime and looking at them makes Eveline's mouth water.

Two silver teaspoons, side by side. Eveline takes them carefully out of the velvet-lined box they're kept in. They're real silver: smooth and heavy in her hands. *Now, they'd be worth a bob or two*, she imagines Ada whispering in her head. But Eveline doesn't allow herself to think things like that. She's not one of those maids who'd slip a silver spoon up her sleeve or into her apron pocket. She's a good girl. Steady, reliable. A hard worker. The sort you can trust.

She warms the teapot, just the way the mistress likes it. It's the new china today: white with a narrow edge of green, and a green and purple picture of an angel with wings, blowing a trumpet. The mistress bought the tea set last week at the WSPU shop on the Charing Cross Road. Eveline knows that "WSPU" stands for the Women's Social and Political Union. Ada says they want ladies to be able to vote just like men do, though what an angel with a trumpet's got to do with that, Eveline can't imagine.

The tea set cost ten shillings and six, a good bit more than Eveline will get in her pay packet at the end of the week. The mistress is awfully proud of it. She can't wait to show it off to Miss Wilcox, though Eveline thinks it's not half as pretty as the old set with dainty pink flowers and a gilt rim. Purple and green don't really go together, at least Eveline doesn't think so.

She spoons strawberry jam carefully into the cut-glass dish. Funny to think this might be a jar that Ada filled at the jam factory. Ada took her there once, to show off where she works: a big, noisy place of rattling machinery, the girls crowded together, shouting out to each other or singing music-hall songs in loud voices. A world away from this quiet kitchen: it's Cook's half-day off, so there's no one here but herself, the ticking of the kitchen clock, the kettle singing on the range. She wouldn't swap it for the heat and noise of the factory, no matter what Ada says.

"You'd not catch me skivvying for anyone! I dunno how you can bear it," Ada had declared when Eveline had first started work. "All that bowing and scraping! *Yes, ma'am, no, ma'am, three bags full, ma'am.* Having to keep your mouth shut all the time! It'd drive me batty."

Ma had laughed at her. "You couldn't keep your mouth shut for a minute if you tried, Ada. You make more noise than a church bell!" She'd touched Eveline's cheek. "But my Evvy's a good girl. She's got herself a good place."

Eveline has always known she'd go into service. "Get your feet under somebody else's table – that's the way to do it," Da always says. But the thing is, she always imagined she'd have her feet under a nicer table than this one, in the dingy basement kitchen of a tall grey house on a grey London street. She thought she'd work in a grand country manor, like the place Ma and Da met when they were young. In a place like that there'd be other people to talk to – scullery-maids and footmen and bootboys – not like here, where there's no one else but cross old Cook, always complaining about her feet hurting or because the fishmonger's sent the wrong kind of kippers again.

In a better place than this, Eveline would be a proper under-housemaid with a fluffy feather duster and a lace-trimmed apron, and long streamers on her cap, and maybe one day she'd climb up through the ranks and become a head housemaid. Here, she's a maid-of-all-work. Some days it really does feel like *all the work* too, when she's up before six to air the rooms and light the range, sweep the fireplaces and fill the coal-scuttles, brush the boots and lug the hot water upstairs – all before she's had so much as a bite of her own breakfast. Though at least here, she's close to home, which means that on her half-day off she can go and see Ma and Da, and Ada, and the little ones.

But when she does go home, Ada makes fun of her print dress and laughs at her cap and apron. "The badges of servitude", she calls them. Ada turns up her nose at the idea of being anyone's servant. "Cleaning out someone else's drain-holes and scrubbing their floors? No thanks!" But Ada's like that. If you say *right*, she'll say *left*. She talks back to Ma and Da something terrible, and at school she used to cheek the teacher until Eveline was so embarrassed she wanted to hide her face behind her slate. She'd been secretly glad when Ada was thirteen and left school, and she had the classroom to herself.

Eveline loved school. She still thinks about it all the time: the neat rows of wooden desks; the smoky smell of the stove; playing skipping games in the playground. Mr Stephenson, their teacher, would pace up and down at the front, reading them the exciting bits of *Oliver Twist* out loud, or telling them stories from history. "Good work, Eveline," he'd say, about a composition she'd written or a map she'd drawn. She'd been the best in the class at arithmetic and spelling, and sometimes Mr Stephenson let her borrow books to take home – *Alice in Wonderland* and *Black Beauty* or a book of fairy-tales with a blue cover. Once she started reading it was hard to stop. She'd want to keep on going all night, but Ma would say she'd ruin her eyes and insist she blew out her candle. The closest Eveline ever gets to a book now is when she dusts them in the mistress's sitting room, where they're kept in a cabinet, behind glass doors.

Ada, on the other hand, has never been interested in books. Not history, nor geography, nor arithmetic either. She couldn't wait to leave school, but she'd flatly refused the place as a between-maid that Ma had gone to such trouble to find her. "I want my independence, I do. I'm going to be a factory-girl," she'd said, and marched off with her friends to the jam factory.

There'd been an awful to-do about it, of course. Ma was upset: she said factory work wasn't respectable, that the factory-girls were rough and wild. Da shook his head and talked gravely about the tough work and the long hours and the accidents that could happen. But Ada didn't give a farthing for any of it. Just like always, she had to do it her own way – no matter how much trouble she gave. It's selfish, Eveline thinks. She'd never want to upset Ma and Da like that.

The mistress's bell shrills; it's time for tea. Quickly, Eveline spoons the tea leaves into the pot the way she's been taught: one for the mistress, one for the visitor and one for the pot. She pours in the water; the lid clinks into place. Then the pot goes on to the tray and she's out of the kitchen and up the stairs, quick sticks, because once she's rung the bell the mistress doesn't like to be kept waiting. But Eveline is careful too: she's still haunted by the memory of the day she took a spill on the stairs and smashed the mistress's favourite vase. She'd cut her hand so badly it bled all over her apron and she'd had to soak it in vinegar to get the stains out. It didn't half hurt, but worse than that, the mistress had scolded her for a full ten minutes and taken the cost of the vase out of her pay packet. She'd been short for a month until it was all paid back, and she'd been that ashamed when she'd handed her money over to Ma at the end of the week. With Da laid off sick, she knows that every penny counts.

Now Eveline tries to keep her hands steady as she carries the heavy tray, laden with teapot and cups, scones and sugar, milk and jam. As she comes into the drawing room, she knows she mustn't bang the door or rattle the tray, because a good maid is always quiet – low-voiced, soft-footed. More like a ghost than a girl.

The room is warm, a good fire crackling in the hearth, even though it's only September. The mistress is wearing one of her new frocks, but Eveline sees at once that she can't hold a candle to her wealthy visitor, Miss Wilcox. If it wasn't for the fact that maids don't stare, Eveline wouldn't be able to keep her eyes off Miss Wilcox's beautiful embroidered frock, her long string of shining pearls, her wonderful hat with feathers in it.

"The National Federation of Women's Workers really have done the most splendid work," Miss Wilcox is saying. Her voice is rich and deep.

"Yes, splendid!" the mistress echoes back, all eagerness.

"And now nineteen Bermondsey factories have given their girls a wage increase…"

Eveline's ears prick up. They're talking about the Bermondsey strikes! Eveline knows all about those, of course. She's heard about nothing else from Ada since the day the girls walked out of the jam factory.

"You should have been there, Evvy. You ought to've seen it! We all went out together – all shouting and singing through the streets. Not just us, but the girls from the biscuit factory and the chocolate factory and the box-makers too. Some of them had their Sunday best on – all rigged out in feather boas and fur tippets and their best hats. Some had made banners. It was like a party!"

But Ma had been furious. "A party indeed! A workers' strike's not just a bit of fun! What were you thinking? You're none of you part of a proper union – you won't get any strike pay. And they'll likely just give you all the sack! We're counting on you bringing in your share, Ada."

Ada just tossed her head. "I know all that!" she said. "But we've got to speak up. We're *workers*, not slaves. Some of the girls are only on three shillings a week and working a fourteen-hour day – that's not right! If the men can strike, then why shouldn't we? We've got to raise our voices – else nothing will ever change."

Eveline had gone back to work feeling sick to her stomach. What would they do if Ada lost her job? It wouldn't be easy for her to find a new one. Money was scarce enough as it was. There were the little ones to think about, and there were doctor's bills to pay for Da.

One long week had dragged by, then another, and still the factory-girls were on strike. When Eveline trudged home for her half-day there was nothing for tea but stale bread and a scraping of dripping. Da looked grieved and Ma had begun to talk of taking in shirt-making to make a few extra shillings. Eveline was so angry that she could hardly look at Ada, who sat with her head held high, as though she'd done nothing wrong.

But at the end of three long weeks, the factory-girls got what they wanted. Ada preened as she put an extra two shillings down on the table for Ma. "See — it was worth it," she said to Eveline. "Two shillings more a week. We got unions now. Better working conditions. If you want things to change, you've got to speak up. You have to fight for what you want."

Eveline tries to imagine what would happen if she asked the mistress for two shillings more a week and has to bite her lip to keep a laugh from slipping out. Her hand wobbles and she splashes some tea on to the tray-cloth. The mistress purses up her mouth in disapproval, but she won't say anything about it now, not in front of Miss Wilcox.

Steadying herself, Eveline sets the tray down on the little table she polished to a shine that morning. Miss Wilcox smiles at her, and for a moment she's not sure what to do. Maids are supposed to be invisible, but she doesn't want to be rude, so she smiles uncertainly back.

"So this is one of your housemaids?" asks Miss Wilcox.

The mistress smiles and nods. She doesn't correct Miss Wilcox. She doesn't explain that Eveline is not in fact "one of her housemaids", but instead her one and only maid-of-all-work. She's happy to let Miss Wilcox think she's got a whole army of servants below stairs, instead of only Cook and Eveline.

"What's your name, dear?"

"I'm Eveline, ma'am."

"And how old are you, Eveline?"

"Thirteen, ma'am."

"Only thirteen? Shouldn't you still be at school?"

"Oh no, ma'am. You're allowed to leave at thirteen, if you've got a place."

"And did you want to leave school, Eveline, and come out to work? Or would you rather have stayed on?"

Eveline is foxed. She senses there's a right answer to this question, but she's not sure what it is. She can feel the mistress's eyes fixed on her.

"N-not really, ma'am," she says honestly. "I mean, I didn't want to leave. I liked school. I like learning things. But you can't keep going, can you, not when you could be earning a wage?"

Miss Wilcox looks at her for a moment and Eveline can't help looking back. "You *could* keep on learning, you know, Eveline, even though you're working now," she says. "There are a number of activities we are putting on for young women just like you, to help you continue with your education. There are classes and lectures you might go to. Libraries you could join. All free of charge. I'll leave some information about them for you."

Libraries! It's a magic word. Libraries are full of books, and Eveline thinks that anything would be bearable — lugging the hot-water can up the stairs in the morning, scrubbing out the chamberpots, even Cook's worst moods — if she had a book she could read at the end of the day. The thought of it is so overwhelming that it's all she can do to stammer out, "I'd like that very much, ma'am. Thank you, ma'am."

As she goes back out into the hall, she can hear the mistress saying, "It's very good of you to take an interest in Eveline."

"It's important to do what we can to help these girls, to give them opportunities to learn, don't you agree? There's a great deal more to our work than campaigning for the vote, of course."

"Of course. Would you care for a scone?"

Back in the kitchen, Eveline knows she ought to be working. There's sewing she's meant to be doing for the mistress, but her thread snarls up and she can't fix her attention on her needle. She keeps thinking about what Miss Wilcox said. *Lectures. Classes. Libraries. Books.*

Before she knows it, the mistress's bell is shrilling again and she jumps up to answer it. Upstairs in the drawing room, Miss Wilcox has gone; the room seems smaller and darker without her in it. Eveline goes to pick up the tea-tray but her mistress stops her.

"Come here for a moment, Eveline. I didn't care for the way you spoke to Miss Wilcox this afternoon. I know she was kind enough to ask you about yourself, but the way you answered her was rather bold and insolent."

"I'm sorry, ma'am," whispers Eveline, looking down at the pattern of carpet she'd brushed that morning. She feels very small. She hadn't meant to be rude to anyone, and certainly not Miss Wilcox.

"A maid should always be *quiet* and *respectful*, Eveline. It's important that you remember that."

Out of the corner of her eye, Eveline can see the printed pamphlets Miss Wilcox has left for her, lying on the polished table beside the tea-tray. The top one has a black-and-white illustration on the cover – it's that picture again, the angel with the trumpet. She can just make out a word: she thinks it says *LIBRARY*. The mistress gathers them up in her hand and then turns back to her:

"You do want to be a good girl, don't you, Eveline?"

"Yes, ma'am," Eveline says at once.

The mistress nods briskly. "Very well then, we'll say no more about it. Now, clear away the tray."

And with that, she quickly tosses the little stack of pamphlets into the fire.

For a moment, Eveline is frozen still. She can see the library pamphlet burning. The angel is swallowed up by orange flame and then turns to grey ash.

The mistress looks impatient. "Hurry along, Eveline." Then, seeing that Eveline is still staring at the fire, she adds, gently enough, "I know Miss Wilcox was good enough to leave those for you, but I'm afraid she doesn't quite understand the situation. I can hardly let you go gallivanting about London by yourself, to libraries and lecture halls, can I? It wouldn't be proper! And all it would do is give you ideas above your station, Eveline, and what good is that going to be to you? Besides, when would you get your work done?"

Eveline stares back at her dumbly. In her head she hears Ada say: *if you want things to change, you've got to speak up.*

Eveline carries the tea-tray back down to the kitchen — still quiet but for the ticking of the clock. The plates are strewn with crumbs now, the spoons sticky with jam. There's a smear of butter on the tray-cloth, and the teacups hold the dregs of tea.

Eveline looks at the tray and thinks for a moment about what it would feel like to throw the whole thing on to the kitchen floor. To see the white-and-green teapot smashed into pieces, tea spilling out everywhere. The sugar bowl shattered. The cups with their angels and trumpets broken to smithereens.

But Eveline would never do anything like that. Eveline's a good girl, isn't she? A hard worker. Steady, reliable. One of the ones you can trust.

Instead, she places the tray on the table and begins to tidy up. The butter and sugar back in the larder, the jam in the cupboard. She looks at the jam pot for a moment before she puts it away. The label is a cheerful scarlet and yellow, bearing the jaunty words: *THE VERY BEST STRAWBERRY JAM. A MOST DELICIOUS PRESERVE!* Its boldness makes her think of Ada. She fills the sink for the washing-up, thinking of what Ada would say if she was here now, all the rude names she'd have for the mistress. She'd probably tell Eveline to put those silver teaspoons in her pocket and walk out, right now. The mistress would have to wash her own precious china and make her own tea then, wouldn't she? That'd show her what was what!

Ada would say she should chuck it in, and come and work at the jam factory. She always said she'd get Eveline a job there, once she got tired of that silly cap and apron. In that noisy place, no one will ever say she has to be *quiet* again.

But the thing is that Eveline rather likes being quiet. She always liked the hush of the schoolroom, the flicker of pages turning, the quiet squeak of a pencil on a slate. She likes the idea of a library, the important silence of all those books, brimming over with stories and ideas.

She rolls up her sleeves and puts the china into the soapy water. As she does so, she holds up the teacup, contemplating the green and purple design again. Outlined in green, the angel stands on her toes like a dancer, blowing her trumpet. Not just an angel but a *herald*, a sort of messenger, picked out against the purple background with the letters WSPU. For the first time Eveline notices that the angel is carrying a fluttering banner. Printed on it in tiny letters is the word *FREEDOM*.

She knows the library exists now; Miss Wilcox told her about it. She doesn't need the mistress's permission, does she? She could find it on her own.

The teacup angel is calling her onwards. *You have to fight for what you want*, says Ada in her head. The thought of it is like a peal of trumpets or the smash of china in the basement kitchen, even though Eveline hasn't made a sound.

ON
YOUR
BIKE
Jeanne
Willis

May 20th, 1894
Spring Street, Boston, USA

Dear Diary,

Well, I'll be danged if I didn't hear the most preposterous notion today! I was out sellin' advertising space to make a few cents while my old man, Max, studied at the synagogue, when here's what I heard tell: those two bigwigs Dr Albert Reed and Colonel Pope, owners of Pope Manufacturing Company, are wagering $20,000 against $10,000 that no woman could travel round the world on a bicycle in one year.

No woman? Like all us womenfolk are fit for is bakin', birthin' and blushin'? This got me so huffy, it set me to thinkin' about what my dear departed ma said when my brother Bennett chided me for not actin' ladylike when I was knee-high to a grasshopper: "Annie Cohen," she said. "Don't you give a bean what Bennett or any boy thinks. You have more grit and gumption than any gal in Boston already. It will carry you far, Bubbala."

It sure will, Ma. I'm gonna get some wheels and go right around the world!

✴

May 26th

I put my name down for the wager – I will travel round the world by bicycle, setting off from Chicago in September. Now all I have to do is get some sponsors to give me some gelt for my trip. What in tarnation could possibly go wrong? I'm Yiddish in a city full of Jew-haters, five foot three, married with three kids and here's the clincher: I have never ridden a bicycle in all my born days. Pshaw! I'm not going to hang up my fiddle over a bitty thing like that. Bennett's wife, Bertha, says she'll mind Malkie and Libby and my boy chick, Simon, along with her own little ones. I guess that's the good thing about two families livin' under one roof, though there's no room to swing a cat with five kids frolicking about. I asked if they minded me leaving them for a whole year and Libs threw her bonnet in the air and said, "You go, Ma!" Simon sulked a little. He says old dames can't cycle no how (I'm 24) and that I'm gonna fall right off my saddle and be sorry, but Malkie pushed his face in the chicken soup and said if *she* was his ma, she'd ride to the moon and stay there and even *that* wasn't far enough to get away from a pea-brain critter like him.

May 27th

Oy yoy yoy! I'm dancing round the parlour with the dawg. I just heard that the folk who run the Londonderry Lithia Spring Water Company have agreed to sponsor little ol' me. All I have to do is carry a billboard on my back wheel and change my name to Annie Londonderry, and they will give me the almighty sum of $100! I told them I'll be truly happy to oblige and, man or woman, I'll be the beatingest rider on the road.

When he heard about the $100, even Simon changed his tune and said, "Bully for you, Ma!" and "When you win, we're gonna be the richest folk in the whole world." Well, I couldn't promise that, but he flung his arms around me and said he was real proud, and Malkie said that when she was a lady, she'd be a brave she-bear like me, not a stay-home ma who never left the yard. Libby said, "You will come home though, won't you, Ma? Only Aunt Bertha doesn't make slapjacks like you do."

I'm really gonna miss my chicks, but maybe it's good for them to learn that women aren't born with both hands glued to a griddle pan.

June 7th

Ain't I the biggest toad in the puddle! Today I took delivery of a real shiny 42-pound Columbia women's bike. It's sittin' in the yard right now under the washing.

I've been practising riding down the lane. Those handle bars sure do have a mind of their own, and my petticoat got caught in the spokes and darn near hurled me over the fence.

Reckon I need to rethink my wardrobe. I'd hate to scandalise the neighbourhood by showin' my ankles so I'll ride out in my long skirt, corset and high collar, and pack some gentlemen clothin' in my saddlebag for later. I have heard tell that a Mr E.C. Pfeiffer pedalled round the globe earlier this year but turned out that was all gum and hogwash. Danged if I know why he didn't make it. Him being a man and all, it wasn't like he was hampered by his petticoat tails. I'm gonna tuck my pearl-handled pistol in my garter and if Mr E.C. Pfeiffer or some other klutz gets in my way, I'm gonna put a bullet through their tyres.

✱

June 15th

Went to the photographic studio this afternoon

and posed with my new bicycle.

I figure I could sell pictures of myself to help fund my trip along the way, and maybe autographs and promotional pins. Old Ma Riley was watchin' me through the window and when I came out she looked me up and down said, "You think you're really something, don'tcha, Annie Kop? Showing everythin' you've got and making a spectacle of yourself in public. Tch!" I just gave her a pitying smile. I guess she's too old to change her views and thinks the whole wide world ends at Spring Street Cemetery.

✹

June 18th

Word is gettin' around about my venture. I'm the talk of the town and while many want to see me fail, seems like plenty don't. I now have more sponsors: the American Ever-Ready folk, who make batteries, the Durham Smokin' Tobacco Company, Lever Brothers, who make Sunlight Soap, and Blocki Perfume. I have so many metal trade signs hangin' off my bike and around my person, when I set off I'm gonna sound like a knight in armour sliding down the stairs on a tin tray.

✹

June 20th

The gossip at the synagogue is this: some of the men, in particular our neighbour, Mr Kleinmann, have been sayin' shame on Max for allowing me to skedaddle off on a bike without a chaperone, but my old man's a new man if ever there was one. He says Mr Kleinmann is an ol' windbag and can go whistle. Max is behind me all the way. He even found me a fine tour book so I could plan my route. It tells all the distances, road conditions, and hotels that offer cyclists a discount. Goodbye, my darlin' Max. Annie Londonderry may be leaving for Chicago tomorrow, but I will always be your ever-lovin' Mrs Kopchovsky.

✳

June 27th

Set off from Massachusetts State House on my bicycle at 11 am, for the official start line in Chicago. Pleased to see quite a big crowd gathered to wave me on my way, along with the press and the big bugs from New Hampshire's Londonderry Lithia Spring Water Company, who fired the starter pistol. I'm feelin' fit and dandy and with a good wind behind me, I am hoping to return to Chicago by early September next year to claim my prize money. I just hope my bonnet doesn't blow off!

✦

June 30th.

I've been riding hell-for-leather in the heat without my bonnet, which blew over a bridge a while back, to the amusement of several little guttersnipes. It is not the done thing for a lady to sweat, but after a long schlep like this I sure was glowing like a horse. I got so dry, I drank Londonderry Spring Water like a fish and as you can't cross your legs on a bicycle no how, I hung on until I hit countryside and ducked behind some reeds to answer the call of nature. It's none too easy squatting in a corset, and, while exposing myself to the elements, a bullfrog hopped down my unmentionables, which I did not realise until I hauled them back up around my waist and heard it croak. I do declare I shrieked – not because I'm afeared of frogs, I just like everything in its place, and as he didn't seem to know his place, I fished him out and flung him in the swamp for his impertinence. Times like this, I wish I was born a man. They sure are lucky, knowin' they can just stand and do their business whenever and wherever they please.

✷

August 5th

I have taken a single room tonight at the Beehive Motel, and am bracin' myself for the next leg of my journey. I am sittin' in the dark with my bruised sit-upon plunged in a bath of icy-cold water. Boy, am I saddle-sore. The man who built my bike didn't have a darn clue about women, or my saddle woulda come with a wide velvet cushion. I have heard tell that lining one's bloomers with cabbage leaves is a cure for the chafin', but, just my luck, cabbages are out of season.

✷

August 24th

Been on the road almost two months, and I confess I miss my home comforts a little, but nothin' compared to how much I miss Max and the chicks. My calves are black and blue from being pedal-whacked and all this exercise is takin' a toll on my curves. I've lost two whole inches off my waist and had to make a new hole in my belt to keep my skirt from slippin'. My bosom is as flat as fried eggs, which means my corset is now three sizes too big, no matter how tight I lace it, and while the lack of bounce is a good thing when I hit a bump on the road, the looseness of the garment makes it jump up and catch me right on the chin. When I'm feelin' low like this, I think of the winnin's, because what little gelt we have doesn't go far, but mostly I'm doin' this to show my girls and my boy chick what a woman can do if she has half a mind to, and that's what keeps me going.

✱

September 24th

Have arrived in Chicago to begin my round-the-world trip. I should be cock-a-hoop but I don't feel so good. I've lost twenty pounds, winter's comin' and there's no way I can make it alive across the mountains to San Francisco before snowfall. I hate to quit, but if I die, that's three kids without their ma.

Now, I know Max would take great care of them but it ain't the same. I lost my ma and pa when I still had milk teeth, so I know how it feels to be an orphan, and no way do I wish that for Malkie, Libs and Si. I think I've come to the end of the road. All bets off, I reckon.

✱

October 4th

Folk say many things about women, but the one

saying I love is this: it's a woman's right to change her mind. Well, I sure have changed mine. Heck, I'm not quitting already! I just hit a glitch, but now I've had a real nice meeting with the people at Sterling Cycle Works. They have a factory and an office in Carroll Street, and I reckon they must have put a huge bet on me, because they want to sponsor me *and* give me a brand-new bicycle!

✹

October 11th

I have my new bike and it's a doozy! It's a men's bike – an Expert Model E Light Roadster – but it's real pretty; ivory and gold with "The Sterling" painted on the frame. It has a single gear, no freewheel mechanism and no brake for lawk's sake, but there's a good reason for that – it's a whole twenty pound lighter than my clunky old Columbia, which will give me a much faster ride for a lot less effort. The notion of this no-brakes thing does make me fret somewhat, but if anyone crosses my path I'll holler like a fishwife, parp my horn and hope and pray they leap outta the way.

✹

October 21st

I am determined to complete my world trip. I have

ditched my heavy skirt, petticoat and rib-crushin' corset, and taken to pedalling in my bloomers. This has given me a real sense of liberation. I feel much cherkier now I can fill my lungs to full capacity the way nature intended and move my knees up and down without getting tangled in yards of flannel. Ten miles per hour is no problem – no one can catch me any more than they could catch a weasel asleep, although the sheriff was so shocked by my "lack of modesty" he did try. That poor man didn't have a leg to stand on. I am not breakin' any law. What could he do except blush and look the other way?

★

October 30th

Since I set off, I've noticed things are a-changin'. I am not alone in wearing minimal attire to assist my safe and speedy ridin' these days. Other ladies I've met who joined the bicycle craze for their good health have adopted the same fashion for themselves, and found the going far easier physically, if not socially. The only inconvenience is that with fall fast approaching, the northerly breeze blows right up the bloomer legs, causin' them to billow like twin windsocks, and while I don't give a hoot if folk laugh and point, maybe I oughta ride in that old tweed suit of Max's before I catch a chill. I don't want a little thing like double pneumonia to put me off my stride.

✱

November 24th

Having followed my route back to New York City, I am now onboard the French Liner *La Touraine*, destined for Le Havre on the north coast. Unless the ship sinks, I should arrive in about ten days, which gives me a chance to catch my breath and plot out the best route.

I hardly recognised myself when I looked in my cabin mirror. My hair is somewhat wild, as I have been wearing it shoved under Max's wool cap to keep it out of my eyes. My skin is no longer fashionably white and my childhood freckles have returned. My limbs, which had become soft and fleshy, are firm and as defined as knots in an oak, and while some might be appalled, I am thrilled by my new athletic appearance. I may not reflect the old-fashioned notion of feminine beauty, but why should there be only one kind? I believe there is something beautiful about a woman lookin' and feelin' strong that need not be described as masculine, except by those with very tiny minds.

✹

December 3rd

I'm spittin' feathers! Soon as I arrived at Le Havre, my bike was confiscated by the French officials for no good reason I can see. They have snatched my money and I have just read the meanest article in the newspaper insulting my appearance, describing me as some kinda down-and-out hobo, and questioning my gender, despite me being a mother of three.

I very much doubt Mr E.C. Pfeiffer had to suffer an assassination on his looks or good character just for riding a darn bike. Nor did he have his choice of clothin' criticised none. I'd like to see those numbskulls ride a bike in a skirt, I really would, and anyway, why should I dress in ribbons and lace to please a man? The line of thinking is that I'm some kind of deranged hussy, a bad mother and generally a blight on womankind. Well, they can go hang. Their blinkered way of thinking has just made me more determined. I want a world where my girl chicks are free to strive for the same things as their brother. What's so wrong with that? I'm gonna go see those officials and tell them straight.

December 5th

"Hell hath no fury like a woman's wrath", or so the Bible-bashers say, and I say good!

I went stormin' up to those officials. I waved my sponsorships and my press clippin's in their red faces, and I made mincemeat outta those boys. By the time I'd said my piece, they were quaking in their boots and could not wait to see the back of me, but I would not leave until I got a sincere apology. After that, I turned on my feminine charm and they gave me my bike back and my money, and to show them no hard feelin's, I gave them a signed photo, which I know the young handsome one hid in his tobacco pouch.

December 9th

I am now drinkin' black coffee outside a little café in Paris and selling my promotional pins for French francs after giving a riding demonstration down the Champs-Elysées. Paris, France is a fine place with more bikes than an onion-seller's convention. Although my French isn't so good, I have been in conversation with flocks of local folk, and the press are all clamourin' to know my story. And if they want to believe I truly am the daughter of the US senator, a wealthy heiress and that I invented a new method of stenography, who am I to disillusion them? I swear half of what they say in the papers is bunkum anyhow, so I figured I might as well give them something a bit more entertainin' to write about. It's called publicity, it's in a good cause and the way I see it, if I embroider things a little, it's harmin' no one and it's fun. Much as I'd like to stay and enthral them with my adventures, I must leave soon and hit the road to Marseille.

✱

December 15th

Dang! Got halfway to Marseille in the pourin' rain and fell off my darn bike. A stray mutt ran out in front of me, I went to slam on the brakes, then remembered there weren't none! Lost control down the hill, hit a rock and sailed through the air like a scarecrow shot from a cannon. Landed, skidded into a tree, tore the backside outta my pants and twisted my ankle. It's fine. I just tore up my old petticoat and strapped it up best as I could. If I rest my foot on the handlebar, I reckon I can still ride to the nearest train station and hitch a lift. Nothin' in the rules to say I can't go part of the way by rail, and when the swellin' goes down I should be ridin' into Marseille within my deadline. I only have eight months to get back to Chicago, so no time to lie down and cry about it.

✱

January 2nd, 1895
Made it to Marseille in one piece. Glad to report my ankle is no longer swollen like an elephant's. Am now aboard a 413-foot steamship to Sydney. I sail from place to place, completing day trips at each stop along the way – Alexandria, Colombo, Singapore, Saigon, Hong Kong – you name it, I've cycled it.

✱

February 12th
I have scrubbed up well enough to dine at the captain's table, and have been amusing the passengers with tales of my wild adventures. I'm not saying that I tell 'em any wilder than they happened, but if someone in first class asks if I was kidnapped by bandits in Colombo and danced with the King of Saigon, it would be rude to disappoint 'em. Mind you, the mere idea of me adventurin' alone is a wild and darin' enough notion for the likes of them. The ladies on board are rich and well travelled, but

as far as their real lives go, they don't seem to look much beyond the horizon. I do detect a little envy in their eyes, seeing as how I'm not glued to a man's side like they are, and the duchess did confide in me that she would swap all her jewels and finery for a similar taste of freedom. Next stop, Shanghai.

✸

March 9th

Have ridden through Nagasaki and the cherry blossom sure was a sight for sore eyes. Cycled through Kobe without a hitch, although I did dodge a bullet and get arrested. By now, my fame has spread to the Orient. The Japanese fishermen threw down their nets and hollered "Annie Londonderry!" as I cycled by, and the workers in the paddy fields stood up and waved. I made good time although it was mighty hilly in places. So far, so good. Those boys who bet a woman couldn't ride around the world are sure gonna lose their wager, I reckon. I am now sailing from Yokohama and hopin' to reach the Golden Gate at Francisco around March 23rd if this ship stays afloat. The sea is mighty choppy tonight and I do feel a little green around the gills, but that might just be because I ate raw fish and it didn't agree with me none. The passengers were fascinated to hear about my tiger huntin' expedition with the Shoguns and how I almost died after being shot and thrown in a Japanese jail, but when they asked to see my bullet wound, I had to excuse myself, run to the deck and hurl.

✱

March 23rd

Arrived at San Francisco on time! The next part of the journey won't be so easy, what with there being a heck of a lot of sand along the way and me not being in possession of a camel. After Arizona, I'll be passin' through New Mexico and El Paso, which sounds like tough goin', but according to my guide book this is where the Southern Pacific Railway tracks offer many benefits to the cyclist. Riders can follow service roads made of hard-packed dirt and stop at shelters built for the train crews, where they can take a welcome bath and have a half-decent meal. Arizona, here I come!

✱

April 27th

New Mexico was a breeze, though I did have a little run-in with a rattlesnake. He wasn't gonna back down, and it was either him or me, so I had no choice but to shoot him and make him into a belt. Things didn't go so good in El Paso. I'm sure I looked left and right and gave a good hand signal, so is it my fault if the locals can't drive straight? It is no exaggeration to say I was darn near killed by a runaway horse and wagon. Luckily I got away with a minor injury and lived to the tell the tale, but *how* I tell the tale when I arrive at Mozart Hall in Stockton to give my lecture is a different kettle of fish. I may have taken a blow to the brain from that horse's hoof, and if my memory does not deceive me, I was coughing up clouds of blood for two days and had to swallow a big ol' darnin' needle to stitch my own lungs back together on the sidewalk. They pay good money to hear me speak and I intend to give them the full dollar. Who would want to hear me bellyaching over a little scratch? Go figure.

✹

July 14th

I have just read in the paper that some folk are presumin' I took the train across the desert, but hand on heart, I declined many a ride from passing train crews. I confess that when I left Albuquerque for Denver, I took advantage of the train across Nebraska, but only on account of the roads being impassable. After the floods, they had been churned into a swamp, infested with alligators with a likin' for chasing bikes, so I did the sensible thing and went by rail. I would just like to point out that in no way did I break my wager by doin' that. I have followed every rule right down to the darn small print, and if ignorant folk are saying I travelled more *with* a bicycle than on one, they can go swing. I would never play a hoax like Mr E.C. Pfeiffer. No, sir. If I did that, I'd never hold my head up high again.

✱

August 20th

There has been a slight annoyin' delay. I'm laid up in an alms hospital near Gladbrook, Iowa for a little while as I have broken my darn wrist. Snapped it like a corn fritter. How was I to know there was a herd of pigs comin' round the bend? I steered sharply to try and save their bacon, but one of the boars got real mad at me and charged my back wheel, and I went straight over the handlebars and didn't land too gracefully. Luckily my bike didn't suffer none, apart from a few scratches to the paintwork. I have a plaster cast up to my elbow, but it doesn't hurt so bad now the laudanum has kicked in. I'm feelin' pretty mellow. The Jewish nurse has asked me to quit singin' as I'm disturbin' the other patients, but when she found out I was the genuine Annie Londonderry, she asked if she could sign my cast. She said I had guts and gumption and should be real proud of my achievement, and that it was an honour to nurse the likes of me. Well, that's the first time I shed a tear on this whole darn trip but only because when she said those sweet words, it reminded me of Ma. She even shared the same name — Beatrice. I wish Ma had seen me grow up and go so far, but I guess if hopes and wishes were hugs and kisses we'd all be happy as hogs.

✱

August 27th

It ain't so terrible trying to steer a bicycle with a plaster cast — look, Ma; no hands! My arm's real itchy on the inside and I'm dying to give it a good scratch, but Nurse Beatrice says the cast has to stay on until I get to Chicago. I'm ahead of schedule despite my hospital stop, so I can afford to slacken my pace and just mosey along. Eat your heart out, Mr Pfeiffer. If you thought ridin' round the world was so darn painful you had to cheat, try givin' birth to three kids. ✱

September 1st

I met two sassy young gals today, nicely turned out and dressmakers by trade. Seeing me riding by, they called out for me to stop and, openin' their purses, offered me a few dollars apiece to give them both a cycle lesson. Seems their husbands refused to learn 'em, afeard they might ride off into the sunset, so I took them to a discreet place and after demonstrating the basic skills, I let them have a try. Well, makin' sure no one was lookin', they hitched up their skirts and took it in turns to mount the saddle, and boy, did they wobble and giggle, but with my sound instruction they soon got the hang of it, as any woman can if she puts her mind to it. They left with a spring in their step, insisting they were gonna save up and get cycles of their own, no matter what their old men said, and I left with a few extra dollars in my pocket. Win–win.

September 9th

I am now on the last stretch of my journey and, barring stray dogs, herds of pigs and plagues of locusts, I reckon I'm gonna reach the finishing line in Chicago almost a fortnight ahead of schedule.

I am delighted to be travelling in the company of two fellow cyclists I met on the road. When I say "fellow", one of them is a fine young gentleman and the other is his fiancée, but Daphne is very much her own woman. She had been followin' my adventures in the paper and said that because of me, she had been inspired to get on her bike, and thanked me for givin' women everywhere the courage to not give a bean what the Old Timers thought we shouldn't and couldn't do. Modesty forbids me to take all the credit for that – and I do have a *little* modesty left, even if I do ride in my bloomers. The gumption has to be there in the first place, but if I helped in my own small way to draw it out and change some rusty old attitudes, it gives me real hope for my girls, and makes the whole trip worthwhile. ✱

September 12th
Chicago

I have ridden over the finishin' line in bright sunshine! The crowds were whoopin' and cheerin' and throwin' their hats in the air like the war was over. I am the first and only woman to cycle round the world and I claim my $10,000! But I haven't just won the money. I haven't just won the bet. I've won the right to call myself a New Woman. I can do anything that a man can do, and it's all thanks to one woman, who never once slapped me down for bein' myself. I did it, Ma!

THE
TUESDAY
AFTERNOON
GHOST

ELLA
RISBRIDGER

I expect you already know what a ghost story is like. Everyone does, and it isn't like this.

For one thing, most ghost stories are made up. This one, as far as I remember, is true.

It didn't happen in history, either. There are no long white nighties or hollow-eyed ghastly faces or rattling chains in this story. It happened, in the grand scheme of things, not very long ago: about fifteen years ago. Which is a long time in some ways, but for ghosts, it's barely a flicker.

And it happened not very far from here, either: about a hundred miles to the north from the little café in which I am writing this down.

It happened in a village outside a market town in the middle of the country. The town was very ordinary, with shops and a cinema, and the village was ordinary too: it had a little school quite close by, and a post office that sold penny sweets and ice lollies, and some new houses and some old houses. It was just like your town. It was just like your village. It was completely ordinary in every way.

You'll read the word "graveyard" in this story and you'll think you're getting to the ghost, but you're not. There aren't any ghosts in the graveyard in this story. The graveyard wasn't even important.

It wasn't that kind of ghost. If it even was a ghost. Josie was never sure, afterwards, if it counted.

It's always difficult, when a story happens to you, to see that it counts just as much as the stories in books. Things in books seem to happen in the right way at the right time, and the people in them always know just what to say. Josie never knew what to say. That was why she was friends with Mara, who always did.

You see, the part of the ghost story that happened to Mara was a proper ghost story right away. The way Mara told it, there was blood, and gore, and all the long white nighties and hollow-eyed ghastly faces and rattling chains you could wish for.

But Josie never saw any of that.

She didn't even see it when it happened to Mara. She didn't say that it hadn't happened – Mara was very convincing – but she never saw it, all the same.

And as for the part that happened only to Josie, well – there had been none of that at all. There had only been a sunlit Tuesday afternoon, with orange and red leaves on the trees, and the light on the water, and a kind of feeling... But that was all.

Mara was all for telling everyone about Josie's part too, but Josie did not know what to say. You remember, she never knew what to say, and she was no good at making things up. Who would believe her anyway? It wasn't a proper ghost story, after all.

If it had been a ghost, you see, it was only a Tuesday-afternoon sort of ghost.

The first part did not happen on a Tuesday; it was a Thursday. It was a warm afternoon in October, and Mara and Josie were walking home.

They always walked home together.

They were not best friends at school. Mara had a school best friend already. Josie had come to the village when she was six, and that was too late. The village school was a very small one, and there were only eleven children in Josie's class: four boys and seven girls. Everybody else had chosen their best friend on the very first day of Infants. Besides, even if someone else had wanted to be Josie's best friend, Josie only wanted to be Mara's.

Mara was the most interesting girl, Josie thought. She had long black hair like a witch, and her mother never made her tie it up. She had gold hoop earrings, and she was allowed to wear slip-on shoes.

Josie's shoes had to have laces and thick rubber soles that wouldn't wear through. Like boys' shoes,

Josie thought bitterly. Honestly, it was no wonder Mara had another best friend for school when Josie's shoes were so awful.

"They are very practical," Josie's mother said placidly. "I want you to be able to run about and jump without consideration as to your sex." This was the kind of thing Josie's mother was always saying, and why it was no good arguing with her about anything. Not that Josie would have argued with her mother in any case – she wasn't brave enough to talk back to adults – but there wasn't any point. Nothing she said made sense. Mara could run and jump much faster than anyone, faster than the boys, and Mara's shoes were lovely, like ballet slippers only black. But Josie's mother would not listen to arguments like this.

That is what Josie's mother was like: always saying things that made no sense, and half the time she wasn't even home when Josie got home from school.

On those days Mrs Curtis from next door had to come round and make dinner out of a tin. ("As if," Mara said scornfully, "we were babies who couldn't work a tin opener!")

Mrs Curtis was rude, and had a moustache; she

cycled everywhere on a tall thin bicycle, and never smiled. She never lost her temper, but she never smiled either. If you were to draw a picture of the village, you would have drawn Mrs Curtis on her bicycle right in the middle of it. Josie did not like Mrs Curtis.

But then, Mara did not like Josie's mother. Josie could tell that Mara was one day going to say something horrible about Josie's mother, and then Josie would have to decide if she was going to be friends with Mara or rude about her mother. She expected she was probably going to choose being friends with Mara.

This was the trouble with Mara. You knew, whatever else you tried to do, you would end up choosing Mara. There was not any point trying to be anybody else's friend when there was a chance of being Mara's friend. Mara was the cleverest, the sharpest, the most *fun*. And she had all the ideas.

Josie, for example, would never have spent all summer in the graveyard without Mara. She would never have found the grave of the admiral who conquered Ibiza, or the little Victorian baby, or the one with the skull and crossbones, or the one with the huge engraving of the motorbike. She would never have known about any of it. She was simply not that kind of person on her own.

The graveyard was Mara's idea, and so was the little red shed. The little red shed plan was the most audacious idea of all. "Audacious" was Mara's new word, and she and Josie were saying it a lot that summer. It meant brave and daring and bold, and those were Mara's favourite things.

The little red shed – and the graveyard – were both home plans, which meant that Josie and Mara did them together. At home they did everything together, and that was why they walked home together. They were home best friends, and that started when the bell rang, and the girl from the other village, Mara's school best friend, got on her bus and went back to her own place.

It was not a very long way home, less than a mile, but it was quite an interesting less than a mile. You went through the playground into the park, and climbed over the fence from the park into the field, and then over another fence and a ditch into the field they called Bodfish.

Bodfish – nobody knew where the name came from – was a tussocky, hillocky field, with ripples in it where the ancient peasants had each had their own ditches to look after. You could jump from ridge to ridge, from tussock to tussock, hillock to hillock.

And it was the best field, partly because of this, but partly because it had two things in it: it had an accidental lake, and a small, tumbledown red shed. (There were also sometimes cows in it, but you could mostly keep out of their way.)

The accidental lake was because Bodfish had a hollow in it. It was a deep hollow, as if a giant had thumped his fist down into the middle of the field. It was about the size of a smallish house, and in summer the hollow was dry, and in autumn and winter the hollow was a lake. All the rainwater (and there was a lot of rain then) collected in it, and did not drain away. It was green and thick and sludgy, and not very deep. Sometimes there were ducks on it.

The little red shed was on the edge of the hollow, at the top of the slope. There was a path from the water's edge to the open front of the shed. It was very old, you could tell: the inside of the walls were made of mud and straw all packed down into bricks. Then someone had put red bricks around the outside, to make it stronger. It was meant for the cows to live in, and for hay to be kept dry.

But some big boys from the other village had come and smashed up the roof. They did this for no reason; it had been perfectly good before that. And the farmer had not fixed up the roof, only moved his hay out, and the cows did not want to go in when there was no hay. So the little red shed was abandoned. It was shadowy and damp, and sometimes even on very sunny days there was kind of a creepy feeling Josie didn't like to talk about. This was, she thought, because it was so far away from anything else; there was nobody about. Only Mara and Josie and the little red shed.

The farmer did not seem to want it any more. It was empty, and nobody went there. Even the big boys had given up going there now they had smashed the roof all in. That was just like the big boys. They stopped caring about a thing once they had broken it.

But Mara and Josie didn't mind. It was because of the big boys smashing up the shed, after all, that it had become abandoned in the first place. And if the shed had not become abandoned, they would never have been able to make the plan.

These were the reasons that Bodfish was the

best field, and that was why even though it was not a long way home, it sometimes took a long time getting there. If you stopped to see what was going on in the lake, or how you might fix up the red shed to live in, you could easily be more than an hour.

This was something Josie and Mara were planning together, and this was what they were talking about as they walked. They had their PE kits on their backs, and their lunchboxes tied to the PE kits, and their book bags tied to the lunchboxes, to keep their hands free.

They were going to fix up the red shed and live in it. They never played at Mara's house, because Mara's mum was very tidy, but Josie was sick of Mrs Curtis, and so they had decided: they needed somewhere else. And the somewhere else was going to be the red shed.

Josie had thought, briefly, of telling her mother about this plan. But Mara had stepped on her foot under the table (they had been having tea).

"If you tell adults anything, they think you don't understand and don't have common sense and then they stop you doing it," she had hissed at Josie, once Josie's mother had left the room. "It's them that don't understand, but they'll never leave us alone if they know."

And Mara was right, of course. It was because they were sensible girls with plenty of common sense that they were allowed to go to and from school alone with just each other, that nobody minded if they were late. It was because of the common sense that nobody said anything about them walking home through Bodfish, past the accidental lake, and past the tumbledown red shed.

Josie had an uncomfortable feeling that the red shed was only not out of bounds because nobody thought they would go in it, but there was no point having those feelings around Mara. Mara simply bashed them down like a lawnmower in a meadow.

"It will be completely fine," said Mara. She had done a good kind of knot in her PE kit bag that kept her lunchbox from dragging in the mud. Josie wished that she had copied it. "It will all be completely fine, so shut up worrying, because it's boring when you worry at me."

Mara jumped neatly from one hillock to the next. She was like a goat, Josie thought. She never slipped, never stumbled. It was quite a steep slope down to the water, and Josie always lost her nerve at this bit. Mara never did.

"Aren't you coming?" Mara was two hillocks in front of Josie by now. "Come on, slowcoach. I want to get up to the red shed. Come on!" She jumped again and Josie followed, three hillocks behind and well away from the slope. The sun was in Josie's eyes. Mara, quicker and bolder, was right on the edge.

"Come on, you baby. Can't you jump faster?"

Josie jumped faster, slipped and her lunchbox dipped briefly into the muddy part between two ridges. She winced.

"Don't bother about your stupid lunchbox," Mara called. "It's only mud." Mara's own lunchbox, held aloft by the clever knot, was pristine. Something moved in the corner of Josie's vision. A shadow, she thought. A girl's shadow? She stopped jumping and looked. But there was nobody there, of course. There was never anybody there. Just her, and Mara, and the red shed.

"Why are you so *slow*, Josie? I'm going to do this all on my own, I swear. I always have to think of everything. It's lucky you've got me, or you'd have no friends. You should be pleased I let you tag along, Josie Jones—"

And that was when it happened.

The shadow was there again, and Josie turned to look, determined to see what it was. And then, when Josie wasn't looking, it happened very fast.

Like the shadow: Mara was there, and then – she wasn't.

There was a high, thin, short scream, and then a heavy thud like a dropped bag of shopping, and then, horribly, silence.

Josie dropped her PE bag and inched her way to the top of the slope.

At the bottom of the slope was Mara, and she was lying very still, face down at the edge of the water.

She's dead, Josie thought, she's dead, she's dead…

And Mara rolled over. She rolled slowly, away from the water's edge, and she rolled as if she was hurt. But she was alive.

Josie sat down on her bottom and slid down carefully. There was mud all over her legs but she didn't care.

Mara's face was very white, and she was covered in thick green slime and black, brackish mud.

"I thought you were dead," Josie said breathlessly,

when she got down. She was about to say, "Are you hurt?"

But Mara said, "You *pushed* me."

"I—What?"

They looked at each other, Josie's face baffled, Mara's crumpled with fury and pain all mixed up.

"You *pushed* me, Josie Jones. You tried to *kill* me. You're a *murderer*."

"But you're not dead," Josie said. There was a ringing in her ears as if she was in outer space and looking at this all happening from very far away.

"No thanks to *you!*"

"But I didn't push you," Josie said. "I wasn't anywhere near you."

"I felt your *hands*," Mara said. "I *felt* your hands on my back and then I fell. Who else pushed me, Josie Jones? Who else could it have been? You've broken my leg and almost drowned me."

"You've broken your leg?" Josie said.

She stooped down to pull Mara out of the mud, but Mara hissed, "Don't come near me. And don't just stand there, go and get help!"

Josie did not know where to go.

"Do I have to tell you everything? I'm the one you tried to *murder*, and now you don't even know how to go and get help? Run up to the school, you idiot, and go along the road in case you see someone we know!"

Josie felt very helpless.

Mara swore at her, words Josie knew she wasn't supposed to know. "Go and get me some help, murderer! Go on the road, not on the field! Run!"

Bewildered and astonished, Josie ran. It seemed a very long way back up to the school, and the road was empty both ways. There was nobody.

And then, up the road from the direction of the school, came Mrs Curtis, cycling very slowly on her upright bicycle. Josie let out a little sigh of relief. She shouted desperately, "Mrs Curtis! Mrs Curtis! Come quick! Help!"

Mrs Curtis pedalled just as slowly as before towards Josie, and Josie ran up the hill to meet her, waving frantically.

"Goodness me, it's Josie Jones," said Mrs Curtis acidly, when they drew level. She put one foot on the ground to stop her bicycle next to Josie.

She did not give Josie a chance to even open her mouth. "Your mother says she's going to be out again tonight and could I help you to your tea again."

She paused, and Josie seized her chance. Before Mrs Curtis could start talking again, Josie gabbled, "Mara slipped – broken leg – in the field…"

"What?" said Mrs Curtis, frowning.

How can she not understand? Josie thought. *Why do adults never listen to anything properly?*

"Mara slipped in the field," Josie said, slower this time. She tried to make sure it was very clear. "Mara slipped down the slope in Bodfish and I think she's broken her leg."

Mrs Curtis made a funny small noise in the back of her throat. "In the field there?" she said.

"Yes!" Josie said impatiently. Why was Mrs Curtis being so very, very slow?

"She slipped down the slope in the field? Into the lake?"

"Yes!"

"Is she – is she hurt?"

"She's broken her *leg*," said Josie. What on earth was wrong with the woman? "I need you to get help, I need help, come and see."

But Mrs Curtis was putting her hands back on the handlebars, as if she was about to cycle away.

"What are you *doing*?" said Josie. "You need to come and see, I need you to help. I can't do this on my own."

"Oh." Mrs Curtis looked very uncomfortable. "I don't think I can. I'm not very well myself. I need to get home."

She did not look well, actually. She was almost as white as Mara had been. But Josie could not think about that right now. Mrs Curtis was the grown-up. She had to behave like it.

"Go and get help, Mrs Curtis," said Josie very firmly. She said it as sternly as she could. She said it like Mara might have said it. Josie never spoke to adults like that. "You must go and fetch an ambulance and Mara's mum. Do you understand? Do you?"

There was a long pause, and then Mrs Curtis nodded, rather meekly. "I'll fetch them," she said.

"Do you promise?"

"I promise," said Mrs Curtis. A little colour was returning to her face.

"You have to," Josie said. "You absolutely have to. She's really hurt, Mrs Curtis. It isn't a trick, or anything. She really is hurt."

"I know," said Mrs Curtis. There was something odd about Mrs Curtis's voice. It was as if something was stuck in her throat. As if she might cry. "I know she is. I will get help, Josie, I will."

"And cycle quicker!" Josie called after her. "Cycle quicker than that!"

And miraculously, Mrs Curtis seemed to increase her pace. Josie watched her figure dwindling into the distance and into the village proper, past the sign that said YOU ARE NOW ENTERING…, and out of sight.

Then Josie turned and ran back to Mara.

She was exactly where Josie had left her, but she had managed to pull herself up to a sitting position. She looked dreadful, and she had been crying. When she saw Josie, she bit her lip very hard to stop crying, and said, "Murderer, what do you want?"

In trying to flag down Mrs Curtis Josie had almost forgotten that Mara thought she was a murderer.

"I honestly didn't touch you," she said. She sat down in the mud next to Mara.

"I felt your hands," Mara said. "I felt you shove me. And then I couldn't keep my balance and I fell off the tussock, and landed on my stupid leg and then I rolled all the way down. Because you pushed me. You pushed me."

"But I didn't," Josie started to say, and Mara said, "I felt it." And then they both stopped speaking, because there didn't seem to be any point.

It seemed like a very long time before anybody came, and then everybody came at once: an ambulance, which stopped at the field gate, and two big paramedics, and Mara's mum, and Josie's mother too. And there were explanations, and Josie waited for Mara to say: *she did it.*

But Mara said nothing. Common sense, Josie thought suddenly. She wants them to know we have common sense. Otherwise they'll stop her doing things even when she's better.

Mara was the one with all the ideas.

And then the ambulance took Mara and her mother away, and Josie's mother took Josie home.

✶

Mara was not at school the next day. Josie's mother picked up Josie at the gate and took her home in the car. After school Josie went to call for Mara, but the door was shut and nobody came to answer it.

Then it was the weekend and Mara did not come to call for Josie. And Josie did not go to call for Mara.

And Mara was still not at school on Monday.

So Josie summoned up all her courage and went to Mara's house. She hammered on the door with both her fists, until at last someone did open it, and when it swung to she said all in one breath, "Is she *dead*?"

"Oh, it's *you*, Josie Jones. We don't want you."

It was the school best friend who had opened the door. She looked at Josie scornfully.

"Is she dead?"

"No thanks to *you*, Josie Jones. She says you pushed her. Everyone knows."

"Who knows?"

"I do," said the school best friend. "And I'm telling everyone. You're crazy, Josie Jones. You keep away from us. You're a murderer."

"But she isn't dead," said Josie.

"You *pushed* her," said the school best friend.

"I did not," Josie said with as much dignity as she could muster, but it didn't matter: she knew it was too late. She could hear it going round already.

The next day Mara was still not at school, and they made get-well cards instead of art.

Josie was doing careful colouring-in when she heard it, just behind her.

178

"Did you hear about Josie Jones?" someone whispered. And someone else whispered: *Josie Jones pushed her! Josie Jones broke Mara's leg! Josie Jones is a murderer!*

She turned round fast and the whispering stopped. But nobody would sit next to her, and nobody looked at her, and as soon as she went back to colouring it started again: *Josie Jones pushed Mara! Josie Jones is a murderer!* Even at playtime, and in the next lesson (which was maths), Josie was sure she could hear it. *Josie Jones doesn't have a best friend! Josie Jones is a murderer!*

She could not think about maths at all. How could she concentrate on isosceles triangles when she had all this to think about? And she didn't have a best friend, unless you counted Mara, and everyone thought she had pushed her. But she had not done that. She was not a murderer. She had been behind Mara by two tussocks, distracted by that shadow.

That shadow, Josie thought suddenly. That shadow! Perhaps there had been someone else up there, and someone else had pushed Mara when she wasn't looking! And perhaps if she could find out who, they would stop saying it! She would just have to explain to Mara and that would be that. She was filled all at once with a kind of hope. She had a plan now. She thought it might be a long time before she got to do it, but she had a plan all the same.

And it was just luck – pure luck – that Josie got her chance the very next day. It was Tuesday.

At breakfast her mother passed Josie the Weetabix, and said, "I'm so sorry, Josie, but I won't be home by three today. After all that business last week, you'll have to stay at school until Mrs Curtis can fetch you. Will you tell the teacher? I don't want you walking home alone."

Josie nodded. Inside her chest something leapt. Already!

"I can trust you, can't I, Josie?"

Josie nodded again.

Josie's mother smiled and ruffled Josie's hair.

"It's hard for you with Mara laid up, I know. She'll be better soon, and then we'll see about you walking home again. Along the road, if possible! No more fields. Do you understand?"

"I understand," said Josie. She ate her Weetabix in three quick bites.

"And tonight you'll wait at school," Josie's mother

said. "Mrs Curtis will fetch you. Will you go and remind her, please? I asked her last night, and gave her the money."

"I'll go now," Josie said. She slid off her stool and went out. At Mrs Curtis's door she took a deep breath before she knocked.

When Mrs Curtis answered, Josie said, "Mum says to remind you you'll need to come and help me with my tea tonight."

Mrs Curtis frowned. "Aren't I collecting you from school?"

"No," Josie said. She had never lied to an adult in her life: another first. "Natalie's mum is dropping me home. But you can help me with my tea."

Mrs Curtis shrugged. "It's all the same to me," she said. "Anything else?"

"I'll be home about half past four," Josie told her. Her heart was pounding in her chest.

"Fine," said Mrs Curtis. She shut the door briskly and Josie climbed into the car.

"All sorted?"

"All sorted," Josie told her mother.

✱

She could not sit still at school. The whispers were louder than ever, but she tried not to listen. I didn't

181

do it, she thought, fiercely. I didn't do it.

She had a plan. She was going to find out who was in the red shed, and who had pushed Mara. She was going to go and find things out. She was going to go adventuring. She was going to go detecting.

At three thirty they filed out. She stuck close to Natalie's family until they were out of the gates, and then, carefully, peeled off. She glanced around. Nobody was looking. Good. She ran swiftly across the park and climbed the fence. Down the other field. Over the fence. Over the ditch. Drifts of golden, reddish leaves were everywhere, and the ditch was full of them. She jumped from tussock to tussock, like Mara, and found it was easier than usual; she seemed to be jumping as fast as Mara, as deftly and smartly as Mara.

She came to the part of the field where the red shed came into view and stopped abruptly.

There was somebody else already in the red shed.

She thought it was Mara at first. But that was impossible.

The somebody else was wearing school uniform – a grey pinafore and white socks, pushed down instead of rolled – and had long hair like Mara's that was loose and wild too. The light shone through it.

Carefully – so carefully – Josie went closer.

It was not Mara. She was like Mara, but not her: the hair was red like the leaves, not black as pitch, and the somebody else was the most freckly person Josie had ever seen. She was about Josie's age, but Josie did not know her, which meant she did not go to Josie's school. Josie knew everybody.

"Did you push my friend?" Josie said, as boldly as she could muster.

The somebody else looked up.

"Who are *you*?"

"I asked you a question," Josie said.

"Why should I answer you?" said the somebody else.

"I don't know you," Josie said.

"I don't know you," said the stranger.

"You're not from here," said Josie.

"You don't have to go on about it," said the stranger. Her voice was cross and rude, as if she'd said this a lot.

The stranger was putting the broken red bricks neatly on to Josie's pile by the door of the little red shed. Then she said, "I do *know*, you know. I do *know* I'm from somewhere else."

"Well, you are," said Josie, and then, on an impulse, added, "I'm not from here either."

The stranger looked at her in surprise, considering her all over. "Aren't you?"

"No," Josie said. "I was born somewhere else. I don't really remember it. Then I lived in other places, and then I came here."

"I didn't know," said the girl. Her voice was less cross now. "Sometimes, it seems like everyone else is from here."

"Yes," Josie said with feeling. It did seem like that. Especially now.

"Is that why that girl said you had no friends?"

"Which girl?"

"With the black hair."

"Maybe," Josie said. "I don't know exactly."

The girl shrugged. "How long have you been here?"

"Ages," Josie said. "Since I was six."

"That *is* ages," said the girl. "I've been here ages too." She straightened the edges of her heap of bricks. "Did you know these bricks weren't here originally?"

"Yes. It's got all straw and mud on the inside."

"It's called wattle and daub actually," said the

girl. She was quite like Mara, Josie thought, but nicer. "Did you know?"

"No," said Josie truthfully. She liked learning new things.

"Was it you who started putting the bricks in a pile?"

"Yes." She decided it was her turn to ask a question. "What's your name?"

The girl seemed to consider this before she answered. Then she said, "Sorrel. What's yours?"

"Josie," Josie said. "I've never met anyone called Sorrel before."

Sorrel only shrugged. "I've met lots of Josies," she said. "Come and help with these bricks. I think we ought to start putting them back around the outside, to protect the wattle and daub. What d'you think?"

Josie looked at it, and saw that she was right; the boys had knocked the red bricks from the outside, and the soft, old, mud-straw bricks were vulnerable and raw, like a wound.

"They need looking after," Sorrel said. "They are very old."

They worked together in silence for a while, stacking the bricks around the soft mud.

"Did you do it?" Josie said after a while.

"Do what?"

"Push my friend."

"Maybe," said Sorrel.

"You really hurt her," Josie said.

"So?"

"You can't just hurt people."

"She said you were tagging along. That was rude."

"You can't just hurt people because they are rude," said Josie.

Sorrel hesitated. Then she said, "Well, I didn't mean to. I thought she'd just fall a bit. I didn't think she'd slip all the way down the slope. It was an accident."

"They think I did it," said Josie.

"Do they?" Sorrel looked quite shocked. "I'm sorry about that. And – and I'm sorry I hurt her. I didn't actually mean to. I didn't mean to at all. I just – I just lost my temper. It's my fault." Sorrel looked as if she might cry. "I honestly didn't mean to," she said. "I wanted her to learn a lesson. I thought about saying sorry but I was scared. I was really scared."

"You should have said sorry," said Josie sternly. "You should have told people it was you."

"She knew it was me," Sorrel said.

"She thought it was *me!*"

"She knew it was me," Sorrel said again. "She knew it was me and she didn't tell, she didn't tell."

"How do you know she didn't tell?" Josie said. "You didn't come out and see."

"She didn't tell on me," Sorrel said. "She didn't tell, and I didn't say sorry. She didn't tell, and I didn't say sorry. I didn't say sorry, and she didn't tell. She didn't tell, I didn't say sorry, I didn't say sorry, I didn't say sorry..."

Josie looked up, and the low sun was in her eyes again. She was blinded for half a second, and she blinked hard against the light.

And she was alone.

"Sorrel!" she called loudly. There was nobody there. "Sorrel! Sorrel!"

But nobody answered. And Josie was still alone in the little red shed and it was very cold, in spite of the sun. She was very, very frightened.

And Josie ran. She ran without stopping, all the way home, and she found when she got there she was crying.

She burst through the door.

Mrs Curtis was sitting by the stove with her

hands folded in her lap.

"What on earth's the matter?" she said in her stern voice, and Josie discovered to her surprise that she did not know what to say. Mrs Curtis passed her some kitchen towel and told her to dry her eyes, and she did. When she had stopped crying, it seemed to Josie for a moment that Mrs Curtis was about to say something special, but she only said, "Well, Josie, there's spaghetti hoops for your tea."

It sounded, in the way she said it, like something more important than hoops. It was comforting, Josie thought, and *that* was not something anyone had ever thought about Mrs Curtis before.

Josie made the toast and Mrs Curtis opened the tin and heated up the spaghetti. Josie slid into her place at the table.

"Juice?" said Mrs Curtis. Josie was surprised – she did not have juice in the week, Mrs Curtis knew that. But she nodded, and Mrs Curtis poured her some just the same.

"I wanted you to know," Mrs Curtis said, when Josie was eating her spaghetti hoops, "why I didn't want to help. To come and see your friend. Young Mara."

"But you did help," Josie said. She did not want

Mrs Curtis to feel bad when it was Mrs Curtis who had got the ambulance and the paramedics and the mothers.

"I should have gone faster," Mrs Curtis said. "I should have come to see your friend. But you see, I don't like to go to that field. And it seemed to me that – well, that history was repeating itself."

"What do you mean?"

"I did something very naughty," said Mrs Curtis. "We used to play in that field – probably all children in this village have done, going all the way back to Adam and Eve. It's a good place to play."

Josie nodded vigorously. It was a good place to play. The best place, she thought protectively. The very best place. It was strange to think of Mrs Curtis playing in it too.

"Was the red shed there then?" she asked Mrs Curtis.

"It's much older than me," said Mrs Curtis. "It was there long before I came to the village."

"But you've lived here forever," said Josie.

"Forever now," Mrs Curtis said. "Ages now. But when I was ten I hadn't lived here very long at all. I came from the town, you see. There was a war on. We were sent here to live, my brother and I, to get us out of the city. I loved it here."

She paused, as if she didn't want to say the next part. But Josie said, "Go on," and she did.

"My friend and I were playing out," said Mrs Curtis. Her mouth was almost closed, as if she was having to push the words out hard through her teeth. "And I did a terrible thing. We were playing at the top of the slope. And I pushed my friend. She was always bossing me about, always faster than me, always better than me. She was always the one with all the ideas. I was jealous, I suppose. She had a best friend. I was always the one tagging behind. I wanted her to be the one to fall for once. And she fell – and she was quite badly hurt, and her family moved away. I pushed her, and she fell."

And suddenly Josie knew. Probably you (the one reading this story) have known for a long time, but remember, Josie didn't know that this was a story. It was just her life, and it was all happening in a muddle of spaghetti hoops and isosceles triangles.

And Josie said, very daringly, "Was her name Sorrel?"

And Mrs Curtis looked very surprised. "Where did you get that from?" she asked Josie.

"I – I—" Josie didn't exactly know what to say.

You remember, she never did. "Did she *die?*" she said, all in a rush. "Did Sorrel *die?*"

But Mrs Curtis said, "But I'm Sorrel. Sorrel was me. *Is* me."

And Josie looked at Mrs Curtis, and Mrs Curtis looked at Josie, and Josie saw that underneath the wrinkles you could see her skin was very fair, and very freckled.

"She didn't die," said Mrs Curtis. "But she didn't come back to the village. I never saw her again. Never got to say I was sorry. She lives in the town now. I wish—" And then she stopped, as if she didn't know how to go on.

"I know," Josie said gently.

She finished her tea.

"Thank you," she said to Mrs Curtis, and she did not mean for the spaghetti hoops.

"I wish," said Mrs Curtis again, and went on slowly, "I wish I could tell her I was sorry. I don't think I'll ever be able to feel easy about it, you know. I did a terrible thing, and I've been sorry ever since. I really have."

"I know," said Josie. She did know.

They sat together in silence for a long time: a comfortable silence. They understood each other,

Josie thought.

"What was your friend's name?" she asked, and Mrs Curtis told her.

I told you Josie did not tell this story before she was a grown-up, and that was not quite true. She told Mara. She thought Mara should probably know. She went to her house the next day, and the other best friend was not there. Mara's mum let her in and did not seem cross with her.

When Josie had told it to Mara, Mara was quiet for a long time. Then she said, "I see." And Josie knew that she did see.

"I'm sorry I said you pushed me," Mara said.

Josie said, "You weren't to know."

Mara sighed. "No. If I had," she said thoughtfully. "I'd never have said it. Pushed by a ghost is a *much* better story."

"Is it even a ghost?" Josie said.

"Probably not," said Mara. "But it will be when I tell it. You'll see. That's the thing about stories. It doesn't matter what actually happened so long as you tell it right."

She brightened. "I've got a brilliant cast though – look at it. You can write your name if you want. Pushed by a ghost, time off school *and* a brilliant cast. I owe her, really."

They thought about this for a while.

And then together they found a telephone directory, and searched for a certain telephone number. It took them quite a long time – days and days – to get the right one, because they could not ask anyone for help. They did not want to tell anyone the story.

And when they had found the telephone number, they rang it. It was quite complicated to explain, but they managed it.

And when they had managed it, they explained, sort of, to their parents, and to Mrs Curtis. There was an awful lot of fuss but they managed that too, and somehow it ended up (a week or two later) as a kind of party in Josie's kitchen, with everybody there.

And a car pulled up outside, and an old lady got out of the car, and she walked straight to Mrs Curtis, and then – and nobody saw exactly how it happened – the two old ladies were hugging and crying. Tall, stiff Mrs Curtis actually crying!

"I'm so sorry," said Mrs Curtis, crying and laughing at the same time.

"It was so long ago," said the other old lady,

laughing and crying too. "It's been so long, it's been so long!"

"Too long," said Mrs Curtis. "I'm so sorry, I'm so sorry!"

"You're forgiven," said the other old lady. "Of course you're forgiven! You were just a little girl! Only ten! A baby, really!"

And Mara and Josie looked at each other, because ten did not feel at all like being a baby to them. And Josie knew that it had not felt like being a baby to Sorrel either. It had felt just as important as being a grown-up person. They were still not best friends – not in any way the grown-ups would have understood – but it didn't really matter. It was complicated. Lots of things were.

And without speaking Josie and Mara linked little fingers and promised not to forget: not to forget any of it, and not to forget how it felt to be ten, and not to think – *not now, not ever, ever,* thought Josie – that the things that happened to you when you were ten weren't just as important as the things that happened to you when you were twenty or forty or sixty or a hundred. More important, maybe, Josie thought, because hadn't Mrs Curtis been thinking about being ten the whole time? Hadn't part of

Mrs Curtis been ten this whole time?

But she did not say anything. It was not the time, with Mrs Curtis and her old lady friend crying and hugging each other, and everyone saying how lucky it was that Mara and Josie had developed such an interest in history, and Mara telling all the grown-ups there that she had read about it in an old newspaper.

That was what they had decided to say to the adults.

But to everyone else? To everyone else Mara told the whole story. Or *a* whole story, anyway.

Mara was right: it didn't matter what had really happened. It was the story that mattered. Mara's story had a white waily figure in a long nightie, and screams, and blood. They are telling it still, in the little village, as far as I know.

That's how you know it was a good one: it went on telling itself, long after Mara and Josie had grown up and gone away.

This is not such a good story. Nobody is going to tell this one in the little village. Nobody tells a ghost story without a ghost, and how could there be a ghost in this story, when nobody died?

Josie was never sure, herself. Like I told you, she

didn't think it counted.

And then, one evening a long time later when she was quite grown up, somebody asked *her* to tell a ghost story.

And she thought about all the ghost stories she had ever known, and Mara who could tell better stories than anybody, and she thought too about a Tuesday afternoon in October, not really so very long ago, not really so very far from here, and a girl with hair the colour of autumn leaves, and the low sun in her eyes, and Josie opened her mouth, and said:

I expect you already know what a ghost story is like. Everyone does, and it isn't like this...

She changed the names around a bit, but it was true, all the same.

THE
OTTER
PATH

Emma
Carroll

★
PART I

Two years into the war, our village ran out of boys – the useful variety, that is, who could handle a team of horses or milk twenty cows before sunrise. We still had plenty of the use*less* kind, the worst by a whopping mile being Derek Patterson, who was in my class at school and whose idea of fun was making girls cry. Last week he'd upset my best pal Mabel by stealing her jam sandwiches. She didn't have much, Mabel, which made it worse.

When he wasn't upsetting people, Derek hunted otters along the river with his dad. Their dogs – lolloping, bearded things with curly coats and husky barks – chased the otters for hours on end, which to me didn't seem a fair fight either.

That spring, with eighty acres to farm, we found ourselves in a tight spot. The healthy men were off fighting the Germans, and as the Ministry of Food wanted more milk, more wheat, more spuds, we needed help on our farm. The only thing we had plenty of was rats, in the barns and climbing the gutters into our roof. There were so many you'd even catch sight of them in daylight hours.

Then the land girls came.

The War Office said they'd send us two strong young women from London with glowing references to help, though even on the day they arrived, Dad still wasn't convinced.

"What do I want with city girls on my farm?" he grumbled. "They'll be as good as useless."

Yet Mum and I were both looking forward to it: having someone modern and different staying with us was bound to liven things up. There had been a farm at Higher Hope for hundreds of years. House, barns, the whole lot was made of grey flint with walls as thick as a castle's, so all yesterday Mum and I did our best to make the place look welcoming. We made up the big front bedroom with its views over the river, and lit a coal fire in the grate to lift the chill. Our land girls, I decided, would be like older, glamorous sisters.

"Imagine it, Cathy," Mum chatted excitedly as we'd cleaned. "Young women who've seen the world!" Lately she'd been reading novels from the library with dashing titles like *Arabian Adventures* and *Queen For A Day*, which she hid inside recipe books when Dad was in the room.

Being Monday – a school day – I wasn't allowed to stay home to meet the land girls, who were coming on the eleven o'clock bus. Still, I was excited enough to wake extra early. Grabbing my coat and satchel off the peg, I'd enough time to spare to walk to school the long way round, which meant cutting across Longhorn Meadow down to the river.

On the bank between the trees was a faint path. It ran alongside the main, well-trodden one, except you almost had to squint to pick it out. It was the sort of path you sometimes saw in fields, made by rabbits or badgers. This one was an otter path.

If you were really quiet, you'd sometimes catch one scampering along it, their webbed feet and fat, heavy tails flattening the grass.

These days, though, you'd have to be really lucky. Otters were getting rarer. We'd not had a breeding pair here for a couple of years, though if you listened to Mr Patterson you'd think they were as plentiful as the rats in our barns.

You could follow the otter path almost as far as the village. That morning, as I ducked under the trees to join it, I was busy contemplating our land girls. Until, that was, I heard a loud watery plop. I stopped. Craning my neck over the riverbank, I caught sight of an animal rump disappearing into the water. The long pointed tail. The wet, sticking-up fur.

An otter.

People said they were pests for eating too much brown trout and, with rationing on, you could get a good meal out of a plate of fish. But I'd gladly go without trout if it meant the otters got left alone.

Out on the river now the water looked still. This stretch of river was particularly deep where it ran under a line of willows. I kept watching. Not moving a single muscle. I counted to one hundred, then another hundred.

Almost.

A dark head popped up. Two round little black eyes glinted at me. Then, a few yards on, a second head. They both watched me like I watched them. Not moving. Not twitching. I almost believed we'd stay like that all day.

No such luck.

Something startled them. A tail swish and they were off. Ripples spread across the river, reaching the bank. Then the water went back to being dark and still.

I waited, hoping for another glimpse. But in the end, disappointed, I started walking again –

faster than before. I wasn't sure how long I'd been watching the otters but I'd a worry I was going to be late for school. And there were two things our teacher Mrs Melrose didn't like: dirty noses and lateness.

✹

PART 2

I was in trouble when I got there. Lessons had started. Everyone was already hard at work on their sums. Though I tried to sneak in at the back, I didn't escape Mrs Melrose's eagle eye.

"Twenty minutes late, Cathy Crawford!" She pointed at the clock on the wall. "You'll be staying behind at the end of the day to make up the time."

I was horrified. "What, *today*?" I couldn't stay after school. Didn't she realise our land girls were coming?

"Yes, today," Mrs Melrose said irritably. "Sit down and get your workbook out."

Everyone was looking at me. That included Derek Patterson, who, despite sitting right at the front with the naughty kids, turned round to smirk.

"Yes, miss. Sorry, miss," I muttered.

Red-faced with embarrassment, I took my seat next to Mabel.

"Where've you been?" she whispered, looking worried.

"Watching the otters," I whispered back. "First I've seen there in ages."

She rolled her eyes like I was a hopeless case. But at least she let me copy her answers.

✹

All day, I kept thinking of our guests. Did they like their new bedroom? Had Dad been grumpy and rude? If he had then I hoped Mum had made up for it with a nice tea of scones and jam. The thought made my stomach rumble.

Finally, at three o'clock, the bell rang. Mrs Melrose dismissed each row at a time.

Ours, being the back row, went first.

"See you tomorrow, Cathy," Mabel said, pulling a sympathetic face.

Only twenty minutes of sums, I told myself. Then I'd go home the road way, which was quicker. At the very latest I'd be back by four.

The last to go were the pupils in the front row. As they filed past my desk, I overheard Derek speaking to his pal Tommy Bell.

"I'm going down to the river, see if I can catch a bit of sport. Da's out with the hounds today."

I felt my face go tight with anger. Before I could stop myself, I blurted out, "Not on our stretch of river, you're not."

It was a stupid thing to say. Straightaway I knew I should've kept quiet. I didn't have any right to say it either: my dad had never stopped the hounds crossing our land. A lot of people in our village followed the hunt for fun. Going against it wasn't good form in our village. And rumour had it Mr Patterson had a temper on him. It was why Mrs Patterson had moved away to live with her sister, so people said.

Worse than that was the way Derek looked at me, a nasty little glint in his eye. He'd be sure to make a beeline for the very spot I was warning him off, the place where the river cut through our fields. Of course he would. He knew I was trying to protect something. He was spiteful and mean, Derek Patterson, but he wasn't daft. *I* was the stupid one for putting those otters at risk.

I couldn't concentrate after that. All the sums I did, I got horribly wrong, which meant I had to do them again until they were correct. By the time I'd finished it was gone four o'clock. As I rushed out of school, I could hear the otterhounds yammering in the distance. The sound got louder when the wind carried it in my direction. So did the blasts from the hunting horn. I felt suddenly, horribly sick.

I should've gone home. Shut the doors and windows. Eaten jam and scones with our land girls to take my mind off the hunt. What could I do now, other than keep out of the way, and cross fingers and toes that the hounds wouldn't find my otters?

Instead I went towards the river. Straightaway, I saw the flattened grass, much wider than this morning's otter path had been. People had passed this way – lots of them, with dogs. The sight of paw prints and boot prints in the mud filled me with dread. Pushing through overhanging trees and wet grass, I started running.

The path was slippery. It dipped down and up, over tree roots, round rocks. I was sweating under my coat. Another half a mile and a stitch jabbed at my side. I slowed up. The sound of the hunt was louder now. Still no sign of the dogs, but they'd been here all right.

By the time I reached the willow trees at the bottom of our meadow, I knew I was too late.

The grass wasn't just flattened, it was *churned*. And down at the river's edge the stones were splashed with blood. I felt completely hopeless. This was my fault.

Hugging myself, I sat on the riverbank. The grass soaked through my coat and school skirt but I didn't care. I just kept seeing those beautiful creatures playing in the water. And now, hours later, they were dead. All because I'd not kept my mouth shut.

I didn't hear the rustling straightaway. Then, fearing it was a hound strayed from the pack, I scrambled to my feet. The noise was coming from the reeds over by the bridge. I relaxed a little, thinking it was a bird – a moorhen, maybe, or a duck. But what appeared was a tiny brown head – too big for a water vole, too small to be an otter. Whatever it was was crying. A sad little noise like a kitten would make when it was hungry.

I inched forwards for a better look. *Oh my goodness!* It *was* an otter – a baby one. Looking for its parents, probably. Which made me sick with guilt all over again.

Now, I knew you couldn't make wild animals into pets. But an otter cub this small would never survive without feeding. And a not-so-distant blast on the horn reminded me the hunt wasn't far away, either.

I inched towards it. The cub was on my side of the river. It looked up at me, mewled a bit, licked its lips. Maybe it was hoping I'd feed it. Kneeling on the bank, I could just about reach it.

"Come here, little one," I murmured.

It wriggled – as slippery as a fish, and strong too. But once I wrapped it in my scarf it settled again. Or maybe the struggle had worn it out. It fell asleep. Little beady eyes tight shut, its nose blunt and twitching.

Not knowing what else to do, I decided to take it home. I was late already. Dad wouldn't like it: he'd say we'd enough work without trying to hand-rear wild animals, so I knew I'd have to keep it secret. I'd hide it in one of our barns and feed it milk from the goat. When it was strong enough I'd bring it back to the river – a different part of it, where the hunt didn't go. It seemed like a simple enough plan.

✱

PART 3

Back in the yard, the kitchen lights were on. The

windows – steamed up from cooking – were open, and from inside came a laugh I didn't recognise. It threw me for a second, till I remembered the land girls and, despite everything, felt a rush of excitement. Then the back door swung open. The smell of gravy wafted out, making me hungrier than ever.

"There you are, Cathy!" Mum stood on the step, wiping her hands on her pinny. "Where've you been?"

"Sorry, Mabel fell over in the lane." It wasn't a difficult lie. Mabel only had one pair of decent shoes and no rubber boots to speak of, plus I was splattered in river mud as proof.

"Get the worst of that muck off you then," she said. "Dinner's in five minutes."

She seemed in a good mood, and when she went back inside the laughter started again. As I'd hoped, the land girls sounded fun. The noise had woken the cub again. It started mewling for food.

"Sssh!" I told it as I hurried across the yard.

First stop, the goat shed. The milk for today had already been collected. Hyacinth, our milking goat, wasn't impressed at being asked for more. Luckily, the few drops I squeezed out of her were enough for a hungry otter. Though the cub didn't want it at first.

"Come on, come on," I muttered, fretting that any moment Mum would be calling me again.

The trick was to rub some on its gums. After that it licked greedily from my fingers, holding them steady between its own front paws. We'd soon run out of milk though, and it was too late now to fetch any more. Out in the yard I'd heard Dad coming in for dinner. The bang of boots having the mud knocked off them, the opening and closing of the back door.

When the coast was clear, I slipped across the yard to the hay barn. Inside were bales, boxes of old tools, rusty plough parts, empty feed bins. And rats. You could hear them rustling, scratching. When I moved a hay bale, two big ones darted out from underneath. Another one ran across the floor. I kept seeing fast-moving things in the corner of my eye. It worried me they'd harm a baby otter.

So, emptying out a box of tools, I tucked the cub inside. Then I heaved the whole thing up on to a window ledge, where I hoped it'd be out of harm's way.

"I'll be back," I told the otter. "Don't worry."

It blinked at me. Then started mewling again. It was still hungry. I'd have to try again later.

✱

Our kitchen was a whirl of people serving up shepherd's pie and passing plates around. The table looked suddenly cramped. One of the land girls — tall, blonde-haired, all legs and elbows — was sitting in my usual seat. Mum made me pull up a stool.

"Don't make a fuss," she whispered to me, though she was looking at Dad when she said it.

The laughter from earlier had stopped.

"Hello, I'm Vera," the girl said as I squashed in next to her. "You must be Cathy." She had a plummy voice and shook my hand so hard I felt the bones in it creak.

I smiled, glad to get my hand back in one piece. "Hello."

The other girl was called Helen. Like Vera, she wore a uniform of breeches and a pine-green sweater with a shirt underneath. She was small, sharp-faced. Neither girl was what you'd call glamorous. I'd seen more lipstick on Mabel's big sister Rita, and she'd never *been* to London, let alone lived there.

"I'm not afraid of working horses, Mr Crawford," Helen was saying firmly. "I've grown up with them."

"In London? Ploughing Oxford Street now, are they?" Dad replied in that half-bristly, half-joking way of his that left you never quite sure what he meant.

Mum shot me a nervous look, but Helen seemed unfazed. "We had dray horses – two of them. Shires. My father ran a brewery."

"Is that so? Well, it's a rat-catcher I'm needing," Dad said.

On the front of Vera's sweater was a gold badge shaped like a shield. Putting down her fork, she angled it so we could see it more easily.

"Rat-catching," Vera said proudly. "That's what I'm specially trained to do. At your service, Mr Crawford."

After what I'd seen in the barn just now, this was such a relief. Dad, though, didn't look up from pouring gravy on his pie.

"You'd better be good then," he muttered.

"Oh, she's good, all right," Helen replied, a wry expression on her face. "She'll happily tell you how she does it too, right down to the goriest of details."

Mum stared at the pie on her plate. I didn't suppose this was the "interesting talk" she'd had in mind.

By the time I left for school the next morning, the traps were set. The goat shed, the hay barn, the stalls where the horses went when it was too cold to turn them out – Vera had gone through each with mind-boggling precision. She'd even been round the house and up in the attic. The traps had to be in just the right place, at the right angle, she said. Where there wasn't space for a trap, she'd left little piles of poison for the rats to eat. Vera told me all this on the back doorstep. She was taking off her coat just as I was putting mine on.

It occurred to me – horribly – that if she'd gone through the hay barn, she'd have found the otter cub. She might easily have heard it. When I'd tried to feed it this morning all it did was cry. And cry. It didn't want the milk I'd brought it, or the crusts from my toast. The noise it made was weaker today. The same couldn't be said of the rats, who sounded livelier than ever, especially the ones in the hay loft above my head.

Thankfully Vera made no mention of the otter. Though she'd clearly seen the worry on my face.

"Those rats'll be gone in no time," she said, patting my shoulder. "Rest assured, I always get my man."

Which didn't reassure me in the slightest.

✷

PART 4

I arrived at school tired and on edge. If Derek even *dared* to brag about yesterday's hunt, I knew I wouldn't be able to hold back.

Yet it soon became clear there was no Derek.

"He's poorly, miss," said Tommy Bell. "I called in for him this morning. His dad said he had a fever and was staying in bed."

"Oh." Mrs Melrose frowned. It made a squiggly line between her eyebrows. "Right, thank you, Tommy." And she wrote something in her register.

"I wonder what's wrong with him," Mabel whispered to me.

I could think of a whole list of things, but said, "Germs from the river, I expect." And it served him right, frankly, for going hunting there in the first place.

"Hope it's nothing nasty like polio or liver fluke," Mabel sighed.

I scowled at her. "Since when did you start caring about Derek Patterson?"

213

She went pink — a nice, fetching pink, not the blotchy kind. I honestly didn't know what to say.

✱

All day I kept worrying about the otter cub. Would the rats find it? Would Dad discover it? Would it escape its box and nibble Vera's poison? This last one being the least likely because the cub was refusing to eat.

Looking at the clock every five minutes didn't help. Nor did copying really long sentences from the blackboard or reading a story from centuries ago about a man called Piers Plowman.

When finally it was time to go, Mrs Melrose, for once, let the whole class out together. There was a mad scrum for coats in the cloakroom. Then another big crush at the school gates.

"I'd better dash," I said to Mabel, before she could suggest going to the post office for mint humbugs.

"You're not cross with me, are you, Cathy?" she asked, concerned.

It took me a moment to realise she was still talking about Derek.

The road way home took ten minutes if you were quick. I ran all the way up Higher Hope Lane, but couldn't resist pausing at the top to watch Dad and

Helen as they worked the horses over in our east field. They were too far away to speak to, yet just from looking it was obvious they'd made amazing progress. What this morning had been a field of winter grass was now furrow after furrow of soil. I couldn't imagine Dad doing it that fast by himself.

Back at home, the yard looked unusually tidy. Someone had shovelled up the horse droppings and swept the cobbles, and the buckets had all been stacked in one convenient spot instead of scattered about like they usually were. There was no sign of anyone here now though, thankfully.

I went straight to the barn. I couldn't see any rats today, but they were definitely still rustling. Not for much longer: Vera had laid a trail of poison pellets across the floor. Every now and then the thick white line thinned where something had taken a nibble. Fingers crossed that *something* was a big fat rat. Still, as I approached the window, I dreaded seeing the box upturned on the ground, the otter gone.

Yet there it was, so deeply asleep inside the box I had to double-check it was still breathing. It looked adorable, curled nose to tail inside my scarf. So peaceful. And very different to the miserable, crying little thing I'd tried desperately to feed this morning.

"You stay right there," I whispered to it, and went off in search of milk.

Waiting by the goat-shed door for collection was a churn of udder-warm milk. What I needed was a cup or saucer to carry it in. For that I'd have to risk the kitchen.

I decided to tell Mum the milk was for me, although it was a rubbish excuse, since I didn't even like goat's milk. As I hesitated at the back door wracking my brains for something better to say, I overheard her talking inside.

"No one's seen him since yesterday," Mum was saying.

"Poor chap." This was Vera. "Have the police been informed?"

I couldn't hear the reply. A chair scraped the floor as someone got to their feet.

"Well, thanks for the tea, Mrs Crawford," Vera said. "I'm off to check the traps, but I'll keep an eye out on my travels. What does he look like?"

"Dark-brown hair, wiry build. He's got a nasty scar on his right hand."

Now I was confused. The person they were

talking about sounded like Derek – especially the bit about the scar. Mabel once told me he'd got it after an accident with a pan of scalding water, which to my mind meant he was clumsy as well as horrid.

Yet Derek was ill in bed – Tommy Bell had said so. He'd spoken to Mr Patterson just this morning. Which meant Derek couldn't have gone missing – not when he was sick with a fever. Mum must've got it wrong.

✹

PART 5

Derek Patterson wasn't at school the next day either. I was torn between enjoying the peace and quiet of it, and thinking he must be really sick. It was odd how fast Mrs Melrose put a lid on it if anyone mentioned him. Then, at three o'clock, just before she dismissed us, she said rather cryptically, "Go straight home this afternoon, children. If you see anyone acting suspiciously, don't approach them."

No one knew quite what Mrs Melrose meant. But as we left school everyone was on high alert.

"Germans," Tommy Bell insisted. "That's what she's on about."

"Nah, there's a spy in the village," said Graham

Watson, whose parents ran the pub. "My dad's been saying so for months."

"Or a plane's crashed in the woods or someone's found a bomb?" suggested Enid Clarke. She was the cleverest person in our class so if we believed anyone, it'd be her.

The ideas quickly turned silly. Hitler was here for a holiday. A tiger, escaped from Bristol Zoo, had been spotted at Higher Hope. There was a murderer at large.

I could see Mabel getting agitated. Tucking my arm through hers, I hurried her out of earshot. As we stopped at the crossroads to go our separate ways, she kept hold of me.

"Something's happened to Derek," she said, straight out. "The curtains in his room have been drawn for two days solid. There's not even been a light on."

I was shocked. "You've been *staring* at his bedroom window?"

Mabel didn't blush this time; she looked too troubled for that. And as I thought of what I'd overheard in our kitchen yesterday, a funny feeling came over me like a spider walking on my skin. Perhaps Derek wasn't sick at all. In which case, Mr

Patterson was lying.

All the way home, it went round and round my head. I couldn't help but think Mabel's hunch was right, though you couldn't just assume things were fact if you didn't know for certain. The best thing to do, I decided, was to speak to Mum once I'd fed the cub.

I didn't get the chance. As soon as I set foot in the yard, Mum whisked me inside to help make an early supper. By five o'clock, rabbit pie eaten, we were on to apple crumble and custard. Vera, not wanting any, had gone outside to check her traps.

I'd noticed Dad was in a rather good mood.

"This Helen's a hard worker," he confessed. "Got a way with our horses, she has."

Helen didn't smile, didn't blush. She spooned crumble into her mouth as if she already knew all this and Dad was the surprised one, not her.

Mum caught my eye and smiled, glad he'd seen sense. Then she cleared her throat.

"Got something to say, love?" Dad asked.

"I'm going to the pictures tonight with Vera and Helen," she said all in a rush. "They asked me to come along and I said yes."

There was a pause. A silence. I stirred my custard,

not wanting to look at Dad's face.

"That wise, is it?" he asked. "What with this lad gone missing and police all over the place?"

He didn't say no though.

"We'll all be together, Mr Crawford," Helen said, sensible, steady. "We won't be back late."

Before he could reply, the back door flew open. The wind caught it, making it crash into the wall. Feet, still shod in boots, rushed up the passage. Vera appeared in the kitchen doorway, torch still flashing, hair escaping its pins.

"You won't believe what I've just found," she gasped. "In the hay barn..."

My throat clamped shut. All the blood seemed to rush to my head. It was as good as wearing a sign round my neck telling everyone what I'd done. I'd gone soft, Dad would say. Gone against nature and proper countryside ways, and what good did it do, eh? You still ended up with an otter who wouldn't survive.

But no one was paying attention to me. It was Vera they stared at.

"He's here," she said, flushed with excitement. "Come and see for yourselves."

*

Vera was right: she did get her man. Outside the hay barn was a wheelbarrow full of dead rats, though that wasn't what she'd brought us to see. Nor was it my otter cub; the box sat undisturbed on the windowsill.

What I could hear was something moving in the hay. And when Vera swung her torch beam up into the hayloft, I saw why. A boy was staring down at us. I didn't realise who it was straightaway because he looked afraid.

"You'd better come down, lad," Dad said. "The sooner we sort this mess out the better."

The boy was Derek Patterson.

"How long have you been up there?" Helen asked. "Are you all right?"

Derek didn't answer. He moved back from the loft hatch so we couldn't see him any more.

"We should let the police know he's here, Mrs Crawford," Vera pointed out. "Is it a long walk to the village?"

"It'd be quicker to drive," Mum replied, looking at Dad.

"Don't ask me, I've got animals to feed," Dad retorted. But he dug deep in his trouser pocket and, pulling out the car keys, threw them in the air.

"Here, catch!"

Vera caught the keys one-handed. No one bothered to ask if she could drive; it was obvious she could. Mum said she'd go with her to give directions, then, to me as she left, "You know the boy, Cathy. He's in your class at school. Speak to him, will you? See if he's all right."

"*Me?*" It was an awful idea. Derek and I had never said so much as a nice word to each other. Ever.

Yet moments later I was the only person still here. Dad had gone to feed the animals, and Helen, insisting a bowl of apple crumble might tempt Derek down, went back to the kitchen to fetch some.

It felt odd being in here, knowing I wasn't alone. I'd not the foggiest what to say to Derek though, so I tiptoed over to check on my cub. My heart thumped a little. I had an awful feeling it might not be still breathing.

The cub must've heard me coming. A little brown head appeared over the side of the box. Then came a chattering noise, a twitching of whiskers. It looked so much better tonight. Happier. I grinned. Yet before I could reach it, the whole box moved, tipped and tumbled off the windowsill. It was only a drop of a few feet, but I panicked. Fearing my baby otter was hurt, I rushed over, flinging myself down beside the box.

Too late.

The box moved. To my utter amazement, what shot out at high speed wasn't my cub. It was a sleek, long, full-grown otter. I couldn't quite believe what I was seeing.

"Where did *you* come from?" I cried.

In a flash it disappeared behind a hay bale. The cub followed right behind. There was a hush. Something bumped against the wall. A bucket clanked. Above me, the hay loft beams creaked with footsteps.

"Going to try and catch her again, are you?" said Derek.

I looked up. His legs were dangling through the loft hatch. Then both feet found the top rung of the ladder. He started to climb down. I tensed, ready to be angry or hardened or *something*. Yet when he reached the ground and I saw he was still in his school uniform, I suddenly didn't know what to feel. He looked crumpled and grubby, and smaller somehow. There was a stonker of a bruise on his right cheek.

"How d'you know the cub's a *her*?" I stuttered, for want of something to say.

He shrugged, stuffing his hands in his pockets. "Easy when you've got the mother here to compare with."

"The *mother*?" I stared, bewildered. "Is that who the adult otter is? But I thought she… I mean… How did you—"

"I got to her before the hounds did," he said.

I blinked. I'd misheard him, surely. The Derek Patterson I knew hunted otters with his dad; he didn't go around *saving* them.

"Don't stare at me like that," he said wearily. "What else could I do? They're the last otters left on this stretch of river."

"But your dad was out hunting that day. I heard the dogs. How did you catch her?" I asked. The baby otter had wriggled hard enough.

"I held my jacket over the den opening, and when she bolted, I bundled her up in it," he explained. "I came back for the male but…" He trailed off.

"The dogs must've got him," I said grimly. "I saw the blood on the stones by the river."

"Oh that was mine." Derek gestured to his face. "I slipped."

Somehow I didn't believe him.

"They're not going to fetch my dad, are they?" he said, suddenly worried. "Because I'll run off again, I swear I will."

The horrible truth dawned on me then. He wasn't ill or missing – not really. The bully Derek Patterson had run away from an even bigger bully. His own dad. And Mrs Melrose, with her notes in the register and her all-day frown, must have guessed as much too.

The barn door swung open as Helen came back in with a bowl of steaming-hot apple crumble. "Get that down you," she said, placing it in Derek's hands. "Things'll seem better on a full stomach."

Derek tucked in, scraping the bowl so hard I thought he'd take the pattern off. As we watched him, it occurred to me I'd just had a conversation with Derek. A proper one that didn't involve making anyone cry.

"You can stay here tonight if you like," I said.

He didn't answer straightaway. When he did there were tears in his eyes.

✹

Early the next morning, before anyone else was

awake, we took the otters back to the river. It was just the two of us, Derek and me, carrying the box between us. We cut down through Longhorn Meadow, then turned right and followed the otter path away from the village as far as we could go.

"Dad never comes this far," Derek remarked as we set the box down on the bank.

"Exactly," I replied.

The mother otter appeared snout-first from the box. She was cautious, sniffing the air, listening, then tiptoed across the grass to the water's edge. The cub bounded after her, all clumsy and rubbery. They slid into the water together. Within a few strokes, the mother had rolled on to her back. She was making an excited, chattery sound, and when the baby joined in, we both laughed. And laughed.

*

Not long after that, Derek moved away to live with his mum. He never did go home to his dad, or come back to school. In fact, I never saw him again. One day after school, I told Mabel all that'd happened.

"Maybe I got Derek Patterson a bit wrong," I admitted. "He was nasty because he was scared."

Mabel nodded. "Remember when he took my

sandwiches? He gave them straight back when no one was looking."

"It's like he was acting tough to try and please his dad. Underneath, I think he was actually rather nice."

"It's when you get to know people that you see what they're really like," Mabel agreed. "Look at your dad with those land girls. He never stops singing their praises."

As usual, Mabel had a point. Vera's rat-catching skills quickly made her famous throughout the district, and Helen was now in sole charge of the horses, who worked better for her than anyone. Meanwhile, Mum wasn't hiding her library books any more. She even persuaded Dad to go to the pictures with her one evening.

The otter path was still a special spot for me. One day in late spring as I followed it away from the village, the surface of the water broke with a line of bubbles. Three otter heads popped up – one smaller than the other two. They stared at me. And I stared in wonder at them.

This time I didn't tell anyone what I'd seen. I didn't even mention the otter path, which, after all, was just a faint track through the grass. Most people didn't know it existed. But all you had to do was look closely, quietly. The rest came as a wonderful surprise.

A bell is ringing. I think this means it's time for breakfast.

A bell! How old-fashioned.

Mum and Dad dropped me off at the farm yesterday evening. They were in a rush to catch their plane so they stayed less than an hour. I'd watched their car lights trail away into the night, getting smaller and smaller, and then, nothing.

"You'll get used to us and our ways!" Aunty Mo had smiled.

"And we'll get used to yours," cracked Uncle Lee.

Maybe I will and maybe I won't. There's a lot to get used to.

So now I'm inside the airing cupboard. My extremely narrow bed has been built out of wooden pallets and my mattress is made of sofa cushions. My clothes are still in my suitcase as there's nowhere else for them to go. But I'm not complaining. I'm the only kid in the house with their own bedroom. I have five cousins. Yes, FIVE. All boys. Somebody save me!

I wrote Marnie a message last night, but it didn't send because there's no Wi-Fi in here.

I look at it now, to remind myself what I'm in for.

Emergency Situation: abandoned with hardly seen relations for two weeks.

In countryside. On farm. Trees/tractors/mud/dark etc.

Five boy cousins aged from 7 to 15 years old. Ben, Barney, Sid, William, Jack. Can't remember which is which.

Uncle Lee and Aunty Mo. Aunty Mo told me not to call her "Aunty" because it makes her feel old but I'm too embarrassed not to.

Why did my evil parents leave me here? Why why why? Miss you forever! How is Canada? Every time I see a plane in the sky I think of you!

I sniff a bit, feeling tears come. I miss Marnie. I rub at my eyes and breathe.

The bell rings harder as I shuffle down the bed and thump at the tiny ivy-streaked window. It creaks open and a delicious draught of air comes in.

From my perch I can see the farmyard, a row of low old buildings with birds flicking in and out from under the roofs, a dirty quad bike, and various buckets and bits of machinery. Beyond the yard is a large modern barn full of black-wrapped silage bales. I know what they are at least. The tin roof creaks as the wind blows.

On the far hill I can see the horses swishing their tails against the flies.

It's July. I've just broken up from school. I didn't sleep well. I had too much to think about and the bed is so small, and it was really stuffy and I could hear the muffled arguing and chatting of my cousins in the bedrooms beyond.

Five boys!

I hear footsteps on the landing, the thudding of feet down the stairs. There's not time to redo my plait so I wrap my dressing gown round me. (It is PINK. I wish it wasn't. In this house of boys, the colour feels like a challenge.)

There's a bang on my door.

"Hurry up, Fay, or it will all be gone."

I think that was Barney. I can't be sure. I'm hoping that he is going to be OK. I don't know any of my cousins especially well. I've only seen them in the distance at weddings. They are farmers and Mum says farmers don't often leave their farms. Her sister is my Aunty Mo. Mum has always said they didn't have much in common.

Anyway.

I tie the pink ties tighter round my waist, lift

myself off the bed, edge along the wall and open the door.

The clamour grows louder as I approach. This is an ancient house with thick walls and probably lots of dusty history. But it's not spooky.

At home I eat breakfast alone. I read and eat my cornflakes to the hum of the shower pump and the whirr of the hair dryer as Mum gets ready for work. Dad would have already left.

It's not like that here.

When I open the door I'm blasted with warm air and smells. Smells of bodies, smells of burnt porridge, smells of coffee and toast. And the noise! A radio playing, loud chatter, a dog barking, Aunty Mo clattering dishes in or out of the dishwasher. The sounds layer over each other.

Uncle Lee is frying eggs. He's wearing a grey boiler suit with mud on the knees. I count twelve eggs in his frying pan, which must be the largest one in the world. And there are many, many boys sitting or standing at the table, feeding like hungry livestock.

One of the cousins has built a wall of cereal boxes around himself. All that can be seen are his pyjamaed elbows. Someone else is reading the paper, the pages held high so I can't see anything of him either.

There is thumping coming from under the table, which makes the breakfast plates jump.

"STOP IT, Sidney," snaps Aunty Mo. "Hello, sleepy," her voice kinder when she speaks to me. "There's eggs, bacon, toast, cereal, juice, tea, coffee…"

"Thanks," I say, aware of many eyes upon me. The eggs in the pan hiss and spit. Uncle Lee grins at me. He's missing a tooth. "Sunny side up?" he says.

I can't speak in front of all these people so I just smile in return and wonder if I'm brave enough to cross the room and sit on the only empty chair. It's beside a huge teenager, who has hair growing thickly on his arms and a smell coming off him like he's eaten a bucket of garlic and run a marathon.

This must be…

"Jack," says Jack. He grimaces "Don't eat Dad's cooking. He never washes his hands and he's been docking sheep."

I hesitate. Was docking sheep anything like docking your phone?

"Sleep well?" asks Uncle Lee, not bothering to

defend his hygiene.

I nod, sit next to Jack-the-giant and bravely spear a slice of toast from a cracked plate in the centre of the table. Jack shovels in a huge spoonful of Cheerios then empties out the box for another round.

He really stinks.

Uncle Lee, catching my eye, winks and opens the window above the kitchen sink.

"How's the cupboard, Fay?" says a high voice. I think I know this one – this is Ben. My youngest cousin. He's small and a little bit chubby, with dark hair and a smiley face.

"Great," I say, realising it's the first word I've said.

"It was full of our sheets and towels, but we reckoned we could turn it into a tiny, tiny bedroom for you." Aunt Mo looked apologetic.

"I love it," I say truthfully.

"Eggs," says Uncle Lee, and flips one on to my toast. It's a deep yellow. It would be like eating sunshine. My stomach rumbles and I remember I was too tired, too flustered, to eat anything when I arrived yesterday. Through all the noise and chatter, someone shoves a dish of butter at me, and from somewhere else the tomato sauce lands near my plate.

Aunty Mo places a mug of tea in front of me.

"This treatment won't last long," says a voice from behind the sports pages of *The Times*. "Tomorrow you'll have to fight for every scrap like the rest of us."

This must be William. He lowers the paper and takes a slug of tea. He is extremely thin, with long arms. His knuckles look like they've been glued on.

He's also wearing a pink and yellow flowery dressing gown. If anything it's more girly than mine. His bony wrists stick out from the lacy hems. He looks the tiniest bit like my dad.

"So then, cousin Fay, why have your mum and dad gone on holiday without you?" pipes up Ben.

"Shhh," says Aunty Mo.

"Don't they like you?" asks Ben, not shhh-ing.

I can't think of anything to say when everyone is looking at me.

"Shut up, Ben," says Uncle Lee. "Her parents don't need a break from her. They're having an anniversary holiday."

I stab my egg. I don't mind my parents going off to Paris without me. But I do mind coming here. I was supposed to be staying with my other GIRL cousins. Ones I know. Stella and Lou. But the whole house got a sick bug and so I've ended up here on the farm in Somerset, in the middle of the countryside, with no Wi-Fi, no shops or buses and all these boys.

"You need a haircut," says Ben, twitching the end of my plait.

"I know," I say.

"Sid had long hair but he kept getting nits," continues Ben. "He had more lice than the dog."

"I see," I say.

"Mum said she should get a flea collar for him," says Ben.

"Well, I haven't got nits," I say somewhat haughtily.

"Got one!" shouts Ben, pinching at my hair.

"Leave her alone, Ben, you little beep," says William, whacking him with his newspaper. "Don't worry, cuz, it means he likes you."

"Great," I say uncertainly.

"You don't say much," says Ben.

"You say too much," says Uncle Lee.

"Do you ride?" comes a fresh onslaught from under the table.

"A little bit," I reply. I lean down and lift the tablecloth. Underneath, a boy about my age sits cross-legged, wearing nothing but old jogging trousers. A plate of toast crusts rests on his lap.

"I'm Sid." His hair is shaved nearly to his skull and there is a smear of jam on his face. "We'll meet you in the yard in ten."

I am instantly horrified. I haven't ridden for years and even then I wasn't particularly good at it. I stopped riding because, Alice, one of Mum's friends, fell off her horse and broke her leg really badly.

She still has a limp now.

"She doesn't have to get on a horse the second she gets here. She might want to come and look at the cows first," protests Uncle Lee.

"She can ride Crispy. He's good with everyone." Aunty Mo clears plates and wipes up spills. "She can do The Race with us."

"Do you want to ride?" asks Uncle Lee. "This lot are all horse-mad but you don't have to be. You can come and help me turn the hay if you like. How old are you? Twelve or so? You look like you wouldn't have much problem driving a tractor."

"She's eleven," says Aunty Mo. "Don't let him bully you into it."

"I'm not," protests Uncle Lee. "I've got a new

tractor. Well, new-ish. Only fifteen years old. It's got a hydraulic seat and a cab radio. The brakes are very responsive; you'll have no trouble stopping," he added.

"Er," I say. Everyone is looking at me.

"Tractor driving is a life skill," says Uncle Lee. "You can put it on your university application under 'interests'."

Was he joking? I couldn't be sure.

"Shut up, Dad, she's coming with us," says Ben. He looked at me. "Hurry up! It's race day!"

"Do you want to?" asked Aunty Mo, looking hopeful.

"I'll do it," I say, and instantly regret it.

I whip off up the stairs feeling excited and scared, and ten minutes later, wearing somebody else's too-big wellies, I stand in the stable yard, watching my cousins dash about leading, watering and brushing horses, and finding hard hats. In the distance I hear the roar of Uncle Lee's new-but-old tractor.

I still haven't done my hair.

It's a bright but windy day and the wind blows shreds of straw over the yard. A small, off-white dog ambles up to me and gazes into my eyes.

"Hello," I say, and a thin line of drool spools

from its jaw.

"We're in here," calls Aunty Mo from the nearest stable. She's vigorously brushing down a sleepy-looking white horse. The dust from its coat flies into the air.

Aunty Mo hands me the brush. "This is Crispy. He's very gentle."

Crispy sniffs me a couple of times, then goes back to munching hay. I set to, brushing burrs and mud out of his coat. I breathe in the smell of horse. It's a good smell, I remember now.

It's exactly a month since Marnie left for Canada. We had FaceTimed every day at first, then twice a week, and last week there had just been an email from her.

HI FEEPS!

SO BUSY!

NEW SCHOOL. LOTS OF NICE PEOPLE BUT NO ONE LIKE YOU. MISS YOU, BUDDY!

THIS PLACE IS AWESOME AND THE FOOD IS AMAZING. OUR HOUSE IS BIG BIG BIG.

THERE IS A TEACHER AT NEW SCHOOL CALLED MRS SIDEBOTTOM! REALLY. SO FUNNY.

LOVE

MARNIE. DON'T YOU DARE FORGET ME.

It was weird at home without Marnie. We'd been in and out of each other's homes all the time and we'd spoken every day about everything. But now she was thousands of miles away forever.

How will I cope without her?

How will I BE?

✹

The dirt comes off Crispy in cloudy, hairy handfuls and settles on my clothes.

I'm wearing new jeans with a purple flower on the leg and my old green T-shirt with more flowers round the hem. Mum likes flowers. Nearly every piece of my clothing has one on it somewhere. I didn't used to mind, but recently the clothes have felt all wrong.

"They're too young for me," I said, when Mum had come home with the jeans.

"But I wear clothes like this and I'm forty!" said Mum.

So I'd worn them. I'm not the arguing sort. But I'd like clothes like Marnie's big sister, Willow. She wears leggings, long T-shirts, hoodies, plain black trainers. Not a flower in sight.

She has short hair too. It looks cool.

Me and Marnie have the longest hair in the school. We've been growing it for years and years. It's sort of a competition, but it's also something that binds us together. I think mine is a bit longer than hers, and she says hers is longer than mine. It grows to our waists. I love and hate mine. Love it because it is thick and soft and on bad days I can hide under it. Hate it because Mum insists on brushing it and that makes me feel like a baby.

"I can brush my own hair," I say.

"So why all the knots?" says Mum.

On the morning after Marnie had flown to Canada, I asked if I could get my hair cut. I know what I want, a bob, to the jaw. But Mum had just laughed and kept on brushing it out.

"Never make big decisions when you're feeling stressed," she said. "I know the day will come when we have to cut your beautiful hair, but not today, not today."

She's always saying that.

And now, brushing Crispy's mane, I tut aloud.

"A horse!" I say. "That's what I feel like."

"You don't look like one," said a voice. It's Sid,

242

leaning in through the half door. I'm beginning to recognise these boys now. Sid is the mostly naked one.

Now he's wearing army shorts and trainers and nothing else.

"Don't you ever wear any clothes?" I ask him bravely.

Sid shrugs. "They only get dirty and itchy."

Aunty Mo walks past carrying a saddle.

"He's never worn them," she says. "He spent most of his toddler years naked. He'd scream the house down if I tried to put him in normal clothes. It was dreadful when he started school and had to wear proper clothes every day. It was like trying to train a Mongolian Mustang." She looked at my flowery jeans and sighed. "I don't expect I'd have had that trouble if I'd had a daughter."

I smile. There's trouble and then there's trouble.

"Why don't you like clothes?" I ask Sid.

Sid shrugs. "Dunno."

"Don't you get cold, and burnt?"

"Yep," says Sid, "but I'm used to it."

"Is it your thing?" I ask.

"My thing?"

"You know, everyone has a thing. Mine is my

long hair and being an only child. My mum's is her deep hatred of butterflies (it's the powdery wings). My dad's is the way cats can't resist him. Everyone has a thing. Is this nakedness thing your thing?"

"I guess it is," said Sid. "And Mum's thing is horses and sons, Dad's thing is tractors and biscuits. Ben's thing is being a pest and taking a very long time on the toilet."

"What about him?" I ask, nodding to a boy cousin (Barney?) who's fitting a saddle on a large white horse.

"He's pretty average," says Sid. "But he's the nice guy, and he loves cheese and banana sandwiches. Maybe that's his thing."

"What about Jack?" I ask, confident my largest cousin was correctly identified.

"Oh, he's good at everything, sport, music, maths, English, everything."

"And him?" I point up to a bedroom window where William is lolling out.

"That's easy," grins Sid. "He's the family weirdo."

"In what way?" I ask.

"Weird ones," says Sid mysteriously, and skips off.

I feel something pull at the hem of my T-shirt.

Crispy is trying to eat me.

"He thinks you're a hedge," says big Jack, clopping past on a large brown and white horse.

I really, really hate this top. Maybe I'll stuff it in a bin somewhere when no one is looking.

I go back to my brushing. I think I'm nearly done when little Ben struggles in with a bucket. It is full of brushes and hoof picks and horse stuff. He sets it down and draws out a pair of gleaming scissors.

"Why don't we cut your hair?" he says. "It would be fun."

I stop brushing. Look at the scissors. Feel my fat plait.

"Don't be stupid," I say.

"I like being stupid," says Ben. "It's fun. Join me."

I feel the end of my plait. The hair wisps over my fingers.

Mum would go insane if I cut my hair. I've been growing it since I was four years old. And people don't just cut their own hair, they go to the hairdresser and pay someone else to do it.

But I've got a crazy feeling inside me, and Mum is hundreds of miles away.

"Just a couple of snips and you would be free,"

says Ben advancing, working the scissors.

"Hand me those right now," I say.

✹

I watch as my cousins thunder out of the yard and through the gate into the field. As I pull at Crispy's head I see all the boys galloping around like mad cowboys. I feel wobbly up here on Crispy's back. It seems a long way to the ground.

I remember Alice's leg.

"Come on, love, give him a kick," calls Aunty Mo, crashing past. She leans over and grabs the reins, tugging Crispy along. He speeds up for a few metres then slows down, wrenches his head free and snatches some grass from the hedge.

The boys wheel round and gallop back to me.

"Come and do The Race. It doesn't matter if you're not a real rider," shouts nearly naked Sid, his cheeks blazing and his muscles taut. "You look like you're about to fall off."

"She won't be able to keep up," sneers Jack, dark and enormous on his frothing horse.

I feel a surge of annoyance.

"We don't have to do The Race. It's Fay's first day," says Barney kindly. He's riding an extremely fat pony with a long black mane and wicked look about it.

"But it's the first official day of the holidays," shouts Jack. "We always do The Race on the first day and the last day. It's tradition."

"Go for it," I say, heaving Crispy's head up and away from the hedge. "I wouldn't want to break the tradition."

"You can just puddle around in the field if you like," says Aunty Mo. "Or follow the trail of dust. It's a race round the circumference of the farm. We end up back here."

I tighten my fingers round the reins.

I think of the trails I've been following in the last few days. The trails of light from Mum and Dad's car, the aeroplane trails in the sky...

"They're all desperate to win," says Aunty Mo.

"But I always win," says Jack.

"Not last year," says Sid.

"That's because I had a broken leg and I still came second," says Jack.

"You had a horse race with a broken leg?" I ask, thinking again of Alice.

Aunty Mo shrugs helplessly. "Jack's like that." She looks at me. "Did something happen to your hair?"

I point down. My discarded plait swings from my saddle like a war trophy. I'd cut it off just below the shoulder.

"Oh dear," says Aunty Mo. "Ben! Did you do that?"

"No," I say. "I did it."

"Oh dear," says Aunty Mo again.

"So who won the race last year?" I ask. I'm learning that if we talk about horses everyone is distracted.

"Me," says William. "It was a hollow victory owing to Jack's leg. This year I want to win for true."

William, I realise, talks funny.

Barney trots back to me. "Can you gallop?" he asks.

"Of course," I lie. I have no idea if it's true because I've never done it. I used to be able to canter and trot. How hard could galloping be? The only reason I hadn't done it is because galloping wasn't allowed in my London riding school. The manège was too small.

"Great! Let's just go for it," says Aunty Mo, who, I know, is as excited as any of them.

"Eat my dust," grins Jack.

"Eat my feet," retorts William

"Going DOWN." Sidney circles the yard.

"No pushing, no trampling, no use of whip," orders Aunty Mo. She has completely forgotten about my hair. "No elbows."

I raise an eyebrow. What is this, rugby?

"ON YOUR MARKS," screams my aunt, "GET SET…"

"GO GO GO," howls little Ben, thundering out in front on his short-legged horse.

So I drag Crispy's head up and urge him on, as my relations belt off round the field.

I know I can't win, but I'm going to be part of this race.

Crispy seems to finally realise that I want him to move, and he ambles at a quick jog after his teammates. I'm bumping up and down and try to remember what I know about riding. Move with the horse, don't let the reins flap and, if in doubt, grab the saddle.

Crispy, seeing his mates vanish into the next field, lets out a little neigh and picks up speed.

"Good BOY," I say. This is fun. Maybe this fortnight with these mad cousins wouldn't be so bad after all. I wonder for a split second what

Marnie is doing. Probably nothing like this. I wonder what she'll say when she finds out about my hair. She didn't want me to cut it either. "We're the exclusive hair gang," she'd said. She said that a lot. She didn't really like me having other friends. I suppose it doesn't really matter any more, seeing as she isn't coming back.

The next field is full of yellow stubble, and already the boys are thundering through the open gateway at the far end. I don't know who's in the lead, but as we fall into a canter and the breeze blows into my face, I feel a surge of joy.

I absolutely do not want to come last.

"Come on, horse," I say, and nudge Crispy in the ribs with my oversized wellies.

The effect is not exactly electric, but Crispy does pick up his pace, snort and kick up a bit of dust of his own.

And the gap between me and the boy at the back — is it Barney? — is decreasing.

As we push through the next gateway, the path winds down a cow-walk into a wooded area, until we reach a stream. And here I find, red-faced and furious, Barney, his trousers all wet, watching helplessly as his horse rolls in the river.

"Is he OK?" I ask, trotting up. (I can remember how to do this.)

"He's FINE," shouts Barney. "He's just rude. I felt him go down, and I had to jump off before I got crushed. He's doing it for fun and to cool down his scabby back."

I watch as the horse rolls and rolls, legs kicking, droplets of muddy water flying over the forest like silver flies.

"Can I go on Crispy?" asks Barney hopefully. "It's not important to you. But it is to me."

I'm about to say "OK" reluctantly, but instead different words come out of my mouth.

"No way," I say and splash past, up the crumbling bank and after the others.

Crispy charges out of the wood and up into the bottom of a steep, steep field. I see the group up ahead, slower now as they climb.

"Come on then," I say, and Crispy pulls after them. I'm gaining on them, and then they vanish over the horizon and as I crest the hill I find myself neck and neck with little Ben and his horse.

"His legs are too short," he wails. "I'll never win on this heap of junk."

"That's not very nice," I say, overtaking.

"I always get the rubbish things because I'm the youngest," moans Ben.

"Tough luck," I say, surging ahead. "I thought I'd got the rubbish horse."

"You have," says Ben. "Crispy is the laziest horse we have." He gets off his horse and tries to pull it up the hill.

"I WANT A MOTORBIKE," he yells.

I lean forward and pat Crispy's neck and he eyes a patch of nettles hopefully.

"No," I say, and we chase the others, cantering along the top ridge of the field. The sky seems huge, and for a moment I feel like I'm in an aeroplane looking down on the fields and hedges as the wind blows over my face.

Crispy is getting into his stride, and I am gaining on the next rider, naked Sid.

We're going faster now and my legs ache trying to cling on. I'm feeling a bit scared as we go faster than ever. This is not a smooth canter, but a fast, drumming move. It must be a gallop.

I'm galloping! ME!

HA HA! I think, and here is Sid, cantering along, looking neat and balanced, not arms flying, feet bumping, like me.

But I am faster.

I keep quiet as we approach, realising Sid has no idea we're here.

I lightly kick Crispy's sides as the ridge starts to slope down and I draw level with Sid and his horse. He looks over, amazed.

"Where are the others?" he shouts.

"Back there," I crow.

Sid picks up speed and for a while we canter side by side, until Crispy's long legs get the better of Sid and his horse and we surge ahead.

"What's got into him?" calls Sid. "He never goes like that for me."

"Maybe he needed a real rider," I shout, and charge off. I seem to have found my voice.

Now I'm travelling fast through rows of Christmas trees. I see Jack, William and Aunty Mo ahead.

Can I do this? Can I?

Crispy snorts, as if reading my thoughts. If I keep going I will, at least, achieve my aim of not losing too badly. But where's the fun in that?

"Come on, Crispy," I say. "Let's show these boys what we can do."

But then Crispy abruptly stops, puts his head

down and yanks at a patch of grass. I nearly go over his head, but manage to stay on.

"Traitor." I glance behind as Sid narrows the gap.

"You're really getting into this!" shouts Sid.

"It's all over," I say.

But then, from nowhere, a jet tears out of the sky. Crispy jerks up, spooked, and belts hell for leather after the others.

I hold on for dear life. This feels even faster than galloping, if that's possible. I'm being shaken all over the place. This is bolting. Even though I pull hard at the reins I can't make Crispy slow down. We fly out of the wood and into a flat field. I'm pulsing with fear and have to grab the saddle so I don't fall off. I'm unable to do anything apart from cling on as Crispy runs and runs, terrified by the roar of the jet.

I pass William and Aunty Mo in a blur.

"Are you OK?" yells Aunty Mo.

I have no idea. I'm frightened, but still feel a jolt of delight as we pass Jack, pounding solidly over the flat field.

"NO WAY!" he shouts.

If I can keep hanging on, everything will be OK. I might even win.

Up ahead I see the farmhouse roof. We are near the end and I am going to win.

The drumming hooves fill my head.

Then I fall off.

It happens quickly. One second I'm in the saddle, the next I'm on the ground, breath knocked out of me, looking at the sky in surprise. I'm bootless — my wellies are still stuck in the stirrups.

Jack bolts past, not bothering to stop.

I cough and wheeze. My arm hurts a bit where I landed on it, but not much.

Aunty Mo pulls up.

"You're so good at falling!" she says, clearly delighted.

"Am I?" I gasp, raising myself.

"Textbook roll," says Aunty Mo. "Clean fall, no getting tangled in the reins. A born rider. Back in a tick."

Then she too kicks her horse and accelerates off, leaving me in the grass. At first I think she's going to catch Crispy, who's now munching the only outcrop of greenery in the shorn field, but no, I should have known better — my mad aunt is chasing Jack.

"THOU ART DEFEATED!" shouts William

as he too passes me by.

As I sit up I hear the growling putter of Uncle Lee's tractor.

"They're all deranged," he says. "Want a ride?"

✶

Back in the yard, I climb down from the tractor, as Crispy sheepishly clatters into the yard. The boys crowd round, congratulating, commiserating. Laughing.

"You don't actually ride very well, Fay," says Sid. "You looked like a sack of potatoes."

"A fast sack of potatoes," I reply. "I was thrashing you until I fell off."

"True," says Sid.

"I'm having Crispy next time," says Ben.

This is a victory of sorts.

Jack struts round, patting his horse and blowing out his cheeks. "Good effort, all," he says. "Especially you, Fay." He gives me a look of amused surprise. "But I won. I am the true winner."

"Congratulations," I say. "And my name is FAITH."

That last bit came out rather loudly.

Maybe I can come back at the end of the holidays and do the last race. Maybe I can beat him next time.

There's always a next time.

"Actually, Jack, you didn't win," calls Aunty Mo.
"I did."

**DISCUSS,
DECIDE,
DO**

CATHERINE
JOHNSON

I ran out of the dark of the tube station and into the bright bank holiday sunshine of the street. I sped up the hill towards the heath and the funfair as fast as I could, dodging through the crowd, the duffel bag with the bottle of lemonade banging against my back. I was meeting the gang, and I should have been there half an hour ago.

Of course, it wasn't my fault I was late. I had to wait until Mum had gone out so we didn't have to have *that* conversation again. I had to get another part-time job, and soon — the paper round didn't pay enough, and unless I could get something else I'd be washing up for the rest of my days in the back of the café that Bubela owned and that Mum worked in. No staying on for my school certificate and no chance of getting the job I wanted. Last time we'd talked about it she shouted at me. No one would want a hairdresser who looked as if they cut their own hair in the dark.

Then I saw my reflection in one of the tearooms by the station and slowed to a stop. I didn't look that bad. The slacks looked great, even though Mum said I looked like a girl from the land army in them. I'd bought them secondhand and fixed them so they fitted. And they felt even better, wide

260

and swingy.

Then I saw my face. I put my hand up to my hair where I'd cut it. Mum had been in tears when she saw me, and after that row I thought one upset was better than two. But honestly, it was *my* hair. And the front where the pin curls had stayed in place had come out the way I wanted. I turned my head round. Maybe not so good at the back.

Somewhere a church clock chimed three and I hurried on again.

I dodged through a group of men and boys, overdressed for the weather in dark shirts and jumpers and flannel trousers. I pushed through them without thinking.

"Oi! Carrots!" someone shouted. "Slow down, ginger!" "What happened to your hair? Fight with a lawnmower!" The men laughed.

I could feel the colour rushing up into my cheeks. When I got home I would cut the rest of it off and dye it black.

I must have scowled.

"Go on, ginger, what happened to your hair? Eh, coppertop! It might never happen! Give us a smile!"

I sped up a little. If I could just get out of their way... I stubbed my foot against an uneven stone and tripped over. I put my hands out to break my fall and the duffle bag on my back swung round and bashed into the pavement before I did. I landed right on top of it. I heard the smash of the bottle of lemonade and felt my front damp.

A gale of laughter exploded all round me. I wished, wished, wished the ground would open up and swallow me whole.

My top – the blue blouse with the swallow print, my favourite – was soaked. I was soaked. I shook the bag away from me. The picnic was ruined. Inside was a mess of broken glass.

I may as well go home right now. Paula and Godfrey would be fed up waiting for me. They might have even done the swing boats without me. You only needed two.

I waited till the men had passed and got up. The bag was a lost cause. I'd empty it out as soon as I found a bin. At least the sun would dry my clothes out quick enough.

I could hear Mum's voice in my head – *Life's not fair, Claudette!* Not bloody fair at all, I thought. I slowed down, kicking a stone into the road.

"You all right?" It was a boy, a tall streak of a kid with blond hair razored short at the sides but with a long floppy fringe. He was struggling up the hill with two placards, but still seemed to think *I* needed help. I must have looked a sight and a half.

He didn't look too sensible himself, given it was summer and he was wearing a dark polo-neck jumper, thick like his mum had made it.

"Going to a funeral?" I said.

He looked embarrassed and pointed up the road to the gang of men disappearing up towards the pond. He plucked at his jumper.

"I'm sorry. That was my dad."

"Lovely man."

"I'm sorry!" He put out a hand to help and smiled. "I'm Trevor."

I almost took it, but then I saw the brightly coloured enamel badges on his jumper. One was a lightning flash in a red circle; the other had two letters – PJ. The penny dropped.

"I'm all right. Thanks," I said, pointing at his placard. "Britain First? And the badge? Perish Judah? What's that about?" He looked interested and went to speak. I put my hand up. "Actually no, I really don't care."

He looked hurt.

"It's free speech. Everyone's got a right to their

point of view!" He sounded annoyed. *Good*, I thought.

"So it's all right to say whatever you like," I said, my voice angry. "Even if it hurts people? Even if people died?"

"Hang on a mo!" Trevor swept his hair out of his eyes. "If you're talking about those camps, that's all lies! It's not been proven."

I think my mouth must have fallen right open.

"The newsreels!?" I said

"They was faked. My dad says that Hitler—"

I cut him off. "We fought a war for years!" I was spitting feathers. "My dad died!"

He sighed – a kind of bored sigh, which just made me madder.

"Of course I'm sorry about your dad," he said. "But the war shouldn't have happened. The Germans never wanted—"

"You're sorry!?" I was ready to explode. My eyes were prickly hot. I set off up the street. At the corner I turned and yelled at him. "Your lot lost! Remember?"

Then I ran away as fast as I could. I wiped my face as I went.

I wasn't crying. Not really.

I found Paula and Godfrey sitting under "our" tree, where the heath slopes down and you can see the whole of London sitting in a bowl underneath you, from Highgate and Islington, all the way to the hills on the other side.

I was out of breath from running, so the words came out between gasps.

"They're here, they're going up to the pond to make speeches, I reckon."

Paula rolled over on to her front and looked across at the city, shading the sun from her eyes with her hand. "I was just saying – wasn't I, Godfrey? – can you remember what it used to be like? Before the bombs? I mean, we were six…"

"I was five," Godfrey said. He looked at me, not quite managing to hide the flicker of shock. "Claud! What happened to your hair?"

Paula turned round and inspected me. "I quite like it. No, honest!" I looked hard at her to see if she meant it. "Well, the front of it anyway. But my mum said I'm not to let you cut my hair." She held her thick plait protectively in her hands. "If you do she says she'll kill you."

I frowned; I really didn't want to talk about

that now. "Forget the hair. You weren't listening!" I looked at them both, from one to the other. "Didn't you hear me? They're coming up the hill right now!"

"Who is? Have you got the lemonade?" Godfrey said. "I'm parched."

"I had an accident." I threw the bag down. They could see it was soaked through.

Paula opened it anyway, frowning when she looked inside. "Who's coming?"

"The fascists!" I said. "You know, blackshirts! All lightning-bolt badges and we-hate-everybody scowls."

"You think he'll be speaking? Their leader?" Godfrey took out his camera. "That could be a story and a half."

Paula gave him a look. "You're a messenger boy, not a reporter."

"One day," Godfrey said, grinning. "Godfrey Munro, *The Times* of London..."

"I don't care!" I was getting angrier. "Why are they even allowed?"

Godfrey looked at me through his camera. "They don't believe it happened, Claudie. There's this chap at work, one of the sub-editors, so he should know better, reckons as it's all made up."

"Well, that's idiotic," Paula said, getting up too, brushing the grass off her dress.

"Why spend six years fighting Nazis if you're going to let them march around saying whatever they like? People died!" I looked at Paula. She knew I meant my dad, her brother, even though I never said it aloud. "It's not right! We've got to do something." I stomped away. I felt fierce, but that might have been because I was thirsty.

"So long as we can go on the swing boats after," Paula called, catching up.

✱

When we reached the pond, there was already a crowd. I didn't recognise any of the men I'd seen on the way from the station. Outside the pub, families were sitting in the sun, drinking. But mostly it was a gaggle of kids in the queue for donkey rides, or sailing boats on the water while their mums sat by the pond, knitting or eating ices.

Godfrey, because he likes to remind us he's earning his living, bought us all lemon ices, and I tipped the broken glass in my bag into a rubbish bin. Paula stroked the donkeys.

"What did your mum say?" Paula asked.

"She says I have to get another part-time job by the end of the summer or leave school and work in the caff. The paper round's not enough."

"Any luck?"

"I want to be a hairdresser, not a waitress! And none of the hairdressers would have me."

Paula made a face.

"I thought the hair would show I meant it. They said to come back when it grew back."

"That's something. Isn't it?"

I lowered my voice. "We need the money, Paula." I threw my lolly stick in the bin. "I don't suppose there's anything going at your newspaper, God?"

"Can you do shorthand?" he asked.

I shook my head.

"She's not really going to make you leave school, is she? Your mum?" Paula looked worried. "I could maybe get mine to talk to her, tell her how important getting a school certificate is."

I made a face. I couldn't think of anything more embarrassing. "I don't think—"

Suddenly two black cabs pulled over on the heath side of the road, and ten people got out before the taxis sped away. They were mostly men, youngish, wearing summer sports clothes, aertex shirts and bomber jackets, but there were a few women too. One had the short curls I'd been aiming for, only she was blonde, wearing an old ATS jacket.

I nudged Paula. "That's the look I wanted!"

We all looked then. There was something about them — not their clothes; it was the way they walked, like they could do anything they wanted, and no one would stop them. They looked like...

"He looks like a film star!" Paula nodded towards the youngest man.

"Some of them look like proper bruisers." Godfrey was dismissive. "And there's a bloke still in his demob suit. Probably only just off the boat from Burma by the look of him."

"OK, not *Picture Post* exactly..." Paula said, but I knew what she meant.

They might not have been smashers, like in the flicks, but you wanted to be them — be their friend, go wherever they were going. There was an easiness about them all.

I crossed my fingers in my pocket and wished that time had done some kind of jump and I was eighteen or twenty — the woman with the curls' age anyway — and had got out of one of those taxis with them. In a moment I had imagined my own future, and it didn't include school. The blonde had a mechanics badge on her army jacket. She took off the jacket and sat on it while she ate her ice.

I turned to Paula. "I'm going to have my own car one day."

"You're going to have to cut a lot of hair!" Godfrey said.

"Maybe I could be a taxi driver?"

"You're an idiot, Claudie! Women don't drive cabs!"

"They did in the war!" I said.

"The war's over!"

I nudged Godfrey hard. "Not for them it isn't!" I said.

From the yard of the pub, I saw the men I'd passed on the hill. All of them had black shirts or black jumpers; some of them had the same lightning-flash badge.

I swear the sun went behind a cloud just at that minute.

Godfrey got out his camera. We watched as they set up a trestle table and laid out books and leaflets. A few of them turned over a milk crate and made a kind of platform, planting their flags and banners – one read "The British League" – behind it.

"Come on." Godfrey began to walk over.

Paula made a face. "I'm staying here."

We reached the table. I could feel the anger in the stares that Godfrey was getting. I wanted to squeeze his hand or something, but he didn't seem that worried. He even smiled a dopey smile at the boy setting out leaflets with titles like "Britain Awake!" and "Jews! Enemy Aliens in our midst!"

Godfrey picked one up and read it aloud. "The Natural Superiority of the European Male."

I realised that the boy selling them was Trevor, the tall boy I'd met earlier. He snatched his leaflet out of Godfrey's hand.

"Careful," Godfrey said to him. "You might catch something and wake up in the morning the same colour as me!"

I stifled a laugh, but Trevor was seething. He leaned forward. "Get out of it, monkey boy!"

Godfrey wasn't fazed at all. "I go where I like," he said steadily. "This is my country too."

Trevor turned on me. "Girls like you. You'll ruin yourself with friends like him! Does your dad know you're mates with a—"

I shut him down. "My dad died fighting fascists like you!"

Suddenly I realised the blonde girl from the taxi in the ATS jacket was there. She didn't see me and Godfrey at all – just picked up a booklet and turned it over. I could see the title – "Jews – Enemies of the Working Man!"

She smiled at Trevor and my heart sank like a stone. "Sooner we can get rid of them the better," she said. "PJ, kiddo!" And she winked at him.

Trevor practically swooned. "PJ!" he stuttered back.

I knew what that meant. Perish Judah. Death to all Jews.

I felt sick inside for ever admiring her. I glared hard.

A man walked across to the stall and told Godfrey to go back to wherever he came from.

"Come on, Claud." God took my arm but I shook him off.

"We have to do something! They can't win!"

One of the men laughed at us and made monkey noises. I saw Godfrey's hands in fists. He spoke low so they couldn't hear. "There's more of them, Claud. And I quite like my camera. And my teeth."

They were all looking at us as he took my hand. I felt so angry and so powerless. It was like a knot in my chest. Why couldn't I do something!

I turned back and shouted at them all. "I'm Jewish!" I yelled. "And you shouldn't be allowed!"

The blackshirts laughed and jeered. Some of them spat at us. Walking back across the road, to the safety of the heath, I felt about two inches tall.

Paula caught us up. "Idiots, the pair of you!"

A man in a black shirt with greased-back hair started talking from the platform – horrible, hate-filled stuff. The blonde woman and the group from the taxi were all listening in the crowd. I wished I was a man – at least, a man who could punch.

"I wouldn't care if they knocked all my teeth out!" I said.

Godfrey wound on his camera. "I think I've got a couple of shots," he said. "Let's go," I said. Although, to be honest, I didn't feel like going to a funfair now.

Before I'd turned round there was a shout. The platform was rushed – it was those young men we'd seen getting out of the taxis. They forced their way through a line of blackshirts and knocked the platform over. Then I saw the blackshirt speaker hit with a punch and go down, holding his jaw. I couldn't help but cheer. Godfrey climbed up a lamppost to get a better look. There was kicking and fighting, and Trevor's stall went down in a flurry of pamphlets. The flags were knocked over.

I dashed back across the road, and saw the blonde woman throwing the leaflets and newssheets into the pond. Trevor desperately tried to save his stock.

"You can't do that!" he said as she aimed another handful into the water. I picked up a pile of leaflets, titled "British Fascism", and threw them too. The blonde smiled.

"You're not one of them?" I asked.

She winked at me then. "Course not, kiddo! Jewish as you."

Then a blackshirt grabbed her arm and swore at her. I tried to kick him hard in the shins, but I had sandals on.

He didn't – wouldn't – let go. I grabbed his arm and pulled and pulled, and then at last I aimed my kick higher, right between the legs. The blackshirt let go and bent double, swearing words I'd never heard in my whole life.

The blonde nodded me thanks.

And then I saw an amazing thing. As the blackshirt came towards us again, the blonde woman drew back her free hand and punched him. Right on the nose. I heard the sound of it! Like nothing else in my whole life. My eyes must have been like saucers.

"Come on, kiddo!" she said, and took my hand. "This is no place…"

She started leading me out of the crowd, but there was fighting all round us.

"Rita Simon," she shouted as we wriggled through the fighting.

"Claudette Nathenson," I said back, smiling so wide I must have looked like an idiot.

"I like your hair." She pulled me through the crowd.

"I cut it myself!" I shouted back over the noise, and she turned round and looked at me again.

"Really?" she said. "That's not bad at all."

And even though everything around us was louder and madder than a Crazy Gang film – I swear I even heard bones breaking – I felt utterly and completely brilliant.

We'd got to the far side of the crowd and heard the cheers as the speaker was hustled away, when there was a whistle. The police! A van had drawn up and the doors were opening. Police in uniform, with truncheons raised, waded into the crowd. I saw two of them grab the man in the demob suit and beat him hard with truncheons.

"You've got the wrong man!" I yelled, but Rita grabbed my arm and shook her head.

"They'll have us in their van and back to the station before you can say Jack Robinson! My mates can look out for themselves."

"But the blackshirts?"

Rita pulled me along. "Not now! Come on."

We both ran across the road and on to the sandy heath towards the trees. As fast as we could we zigzagged and scrambled down the slope between the tree roots until we came to the road that led west.

"The police reckon it's our fault for shutting them down. So we're the ones who get nicked, not the fascists."

"That's so unfair!"

"Tell me something I don't know!"

We kept running until we'd come out of the trees and reached the edge of the funfair. There was the sound of the carousel and the crowds of people walking around, like nothing out of the usual was happening just a few hundred yards away.

Rita still looked wary, scanning the crowd. She took off her jacket and bundled it under her arm.

"If you see a copper, split up and run."

"Who are you?" I said. "You and your friends?"

"The 43 Group. If the police won't stop those people then we have to. Honestly, all these people sitting round saying something should be done, and doing nothing! We're different. We discuss, decide and then do something!"

"Were you all in the army?"

She shrugged. "Most of us. There's a few that were too young – printers, hairdressers…"

"Hairdressers?" I said. "You know a real hairdresser?"

She smiled and ran her hand over her blonde hair. "You don't get fashion like this on the ration! There's a bloke in the group, he's not much older than you."

My mind was galloping along at top speed. She put her arm through mine.

"I expect Vidal could finish your 'do off, especially when I tell him how good you are at kicking Nazis…"

✱

I didn't find Paula and Godfrey until teatime. When I saw them on the swing boats, Paula stood up waving. "We were so worried!" she said as she climbed down. I still felt like I was walking on air. I knew I was smiling a mile wide, because my face hurt with it.

Paula gave me a hug. "We thought the police had carted you off to a cell, or the blackshirts had knocked you for six."

"Why are you smiling like that?" Godfrey asked.

"Cos I'm not going to be leaving school. I've got a job – weekends and Thursday night after school. At a swanky salon in Mayfair with Rita's friend."

Paula hugged me so hard my feet left the ground.

"It's just sweeping up!" I said once she'd put me down. "But I can learn. And Vidal said I showed promise, and he said he'll neaten it up round the back for me before I start."

"Vidal? Funny name!" Godfrey said, making a face.

"Not like God at all then..." Paula said, throwing a clump of grass at him.

"Rita says he's really good. He did her hair," I said.

Paula nodded. "She looked dreamy."

"Can't wait till I tell Mum," I said, putting my arm through Paula's. "No more washing up. No more Bubela telling me not to wear slacks."

"You've still got to go back to school," Godfrey said, and he ran a little ahead and got out his camera.

"You know what?" I said. "I'm even looking forward to another year of school."

Godfrey held up his camera. "Say cheese!"

Me and Paula made the silliest faces.

Then I had an idea. I jumped up on a fallen tree trunk. "Take this one, God!" I said, and swung my leg high like a Windmill girl. "I am Claudette Nathenson and this is how you kick out fascists!"

The 43 Group were a real organisation, begun by young Jewish ex-servicemen who returned from fighting overseas to find that inciting hatred was quite legal on the streets of Britain. They decided not to stand by, but to actively break up meetings of fascist organisations who were free to speak on street corners and at meetings all over London. The organisation grew to include young people who'd been too young to join up, and one of these was Vidal Sassoon, one of the most famous hair stylists of the twentieth century. Rita Simon isn't real, but the group had female and gentile members too.